EMI PINTO

HARPER

An Imprint of HarperCollinsPublishers

Library of Congress Control Number: 2023932839
ISBN 978-0-06-327572-0

Typography by Torborg Davern
23 24 25 26 27 LBC 5 4 3 2 1

First Edition

To Avo, Adam,
and my darling Lilou

PROLOGUE

The Gingerbread Sisters

The glittery streamers on Gretta's handlebars flew straight back like shooting stars as she zipped down the gravel road.

At this speed, no ghost was going to get the best of her.

She stood and leaned forward to meet the hill, pedaling harder than ever as the forest pressed in on either side—thick and dark and full of whispers. Her breath came out in small puffs. Sweat dripped off her thick red curls and mosquitoes whined as dusk turned to night. But she couldn't slow down. Time was running out.

Gretta turned the corner, reaching the top of the hill road as it curved back down. The turnoff was close. And then something cold tugged at her handlebars.

The bike—gingerbread-brown with a lick of pink icing down its neck—swerved, but she held on tight, her feet pedaling as fast as possible.

The handlebars jerked again, but she squeezed her fingers around them in a vise grip.

I don't think so!

The forest of scaly trunks and emerald moss quivered in her peripheral, and it almost looked like eyes blinking. Suddenly, the gravel path seemed to stretch out endlessly, the turnoff gone as if it had never existed. Cold sweat ran down her back and her pulse drummed in her ears.

Gingersnaps! Gretta skidded to a halt, letting the bike fall to the ground in a cloud of dust and streamers. She turned away from the road and squinted into the forest, at the small shimmering patches as blue as her overalls. The lake was near. And so was her sister.

Gretta plunged into the woods, ignoring the branches whipping at her arms and legs. Dead leaves crinkled and twigs snapped, and the patches of blue grew bigger until she was stepping on grass. The familiar shadow of the family cottage rose up against the lake, where a single figure was making its way to the edge of the dock toward a waiting, empty canoe. A girl in a burnt-orange nightie.

Gretta gulped, her ears ringing. She was out of time. The grass slipped away under her feet as she raced across the lawn. Past the firepit. Over the discarded towels left from an afternoon of swimming.

The eerie call of a loon echoed across the water.

Her feet sank slightly in the gray sand but it didn't slow her. She leaped onto the dock as the girl bent toward the canoe, fingers grazing the metal.

"Hanna!"

Gretta wrapped her arms around her sister and they fell backward, hitting the dock. Pain flared up her elbows and through her arms. And then Hanna shook awake, frowning at her surroundings. There was a glimmer in her eyes, like a reflection of someone else, fading with each flutter of her eyelashes. Gretta kept her arms around her sister as her breathing slowed. Safe. They were safe.

For now.

Gretta stuck her chin out at the lake and wrinkled her nose. *Nice try.* The scent of gingerbread wafted in as the trees swayed in a warm breeze. She curled her fingers into fists, hiding the dough encrusted under her nails, and tilted her head toward her sister until their foreheads touched.

"I won't let anything happen to you. I promise."

· 1 ·

Call-Up-a-Storm

The moment the car's tires turned onto the gravel path, Bee's phone lost reception. She watched in dismay as her last text remained unsent, right before the bejeweled case flew out of her hands from the force of her father's not-so-spectacular driving.

The car made a sharp right and skidded into the beginnings of the spidery gravel maze of cottage country roads. Luggage thunked into the cooler, the cooler rolled into the pillows, and one ninety-year-old grandmother squished Bee against the window.

"Storm Lake," Mr. Bakshi read from the road sign. "See, I told you I knew where to turn," he boomed, fiddling with the button to lower his window and managing to lower them all instead. "Did you know this lake only recently got cleared of toxic blue-green algae? Turns the water a beautiful turquoise but will make you sicker than a dog."

The warm, smelly breeze of garbage day hit Bee with full force, robbing the vehicle of air-conditioning and drenching her already frizzy hair with lake humidity in less than a second.

"Dad, it stinks!" She wrinkled her nose as they rolled forward into the trees' shadows. Small mounds of plastic bags and discarded yard trimmings lined the gravel road, ready for the weekly cottage garbage pickup.

"You'll get used to it." He fixed his wide-brimmed fishing hat, pushed his glasses back up his crooked nose, and grinned, making his long face even longer. "Speaking of unwanted smells, did you know a skunk's spray is highly flammable? Good to know if we're having trouble lighting up the campfire, am I right?"

Bee huffed, letting one arm hang out of the window to catch the air between her fingers as the car zipped past the tree line and into the forest. It seemed there was no escape from either the stink, or her dad's weird little factoids.

"You, keep an eye out for treasure." Mrs. Bakshi caught Bee's gaze in the side-view mirror, her long dark hair splaying over her shoulders and framing a perfectly round face. "You wouldn't believe the stuff people throw out. Such a good deal."

Bee's mom stared out the window with enthusiastic

curiosity, as if any minute she'd fall in love with a discarded pile alongside the road. If there was a prize for Most Embarrassing Things Parents Say, Bee's mom would be the undisputed champion.

"Mom, it's not a 'good deal,' it's *garbage*." Bee rolled her eyes, but her mom had turned to her dad.

"And you." She frowned at him. "You call that *knowing* where to turn?" Mrs. Bakshi fumed. "You're lucky my mother isn't chewing you out!"

With her warm complexion, almond eyes, and strong yogi shoulders, she had the vague semblance of an Amazonian princess. An angry Amazonian princess. Because apart from her love of a good deal, she cared *a lot* about the well-being of her family.

"You all right back there?" Bee's mom twisted in her seat, looking in the general direction of where Bee and one little old Granny should have been seated.

Instead, a wrinkled hand poked out from under a mound of displaced pillows, cooler, luggage, and books (according to Bee's mom, bringing a large collection of mystery novels was essential to any successful summer getaway).

"I'm here!" Granny's shaky voice sounded.

"Yup, we're all good," Bee added.

"Oh my gosh." Bee's mom shook her head. "Binita. Binita, dear, do something about the mess back there before you suffocate to death."

"It's fine, leave me here to die," Granny cooed,

before breaking into a poor rendition of "Memory" from the musical *Cats*.

Mrs. Bakshi clicked her tongue on the roof of her mouth. "Binita!"

"I prefer Bee, Mom, *Bee*. Not *Binita*."

Bee sighed, retrieving the cooler and pillows and books, as well as her misplaced phone, and gave Granny's hand a squeeze. Her wispy white hair sat above large sunglasses and deep folds of warm brown skin. It was difficult to believe that once upon a time, Granny had been strong, brave, and fearless. And young.

Granny smiled her thanks without breaking off her song, and Bee returned her gaze to her phone, the large plastic jewels reflecting any ounce of available light like a disco ball.

If you'd met her a few years earlier, Bee wouldn't have been caught dead with such a sparkly accessory. With insufferably frizzy hair and thick-rimmed glasses and blotchy tan skin, Bee's only iota of hope to fit in with her peers was to blend into the background. Which wasn't easy when all your clothes were hand-me-downs from your glitter-obsessed cousin. But everything had changed when she met her bestie, Kitty O'Donnell, who was *obsessed* with shiny. So, obviously, twelve-year-old Bee became a fan, too. And when Kitty decided their cell phones needed a makeover, Bee had immediately pulled out the superglue and crafting gems.

"Are you still on that phone?" her dad chided from

the rearview mirror, raising his bushy brows up into the brim of his hat. "This week of family time on Storm Lake will do you a world of good, you'll see. Did you know it's called Storm Lake because of the loons?"

Ever since he decided to go back to school, Bee's father had developed a fascination with collecting new and random trivia about the country's wildlife. Which he had the unfortunate habit of sprinkling throughout all his conversations, until Bee's head was full to bursting from them. And facts about skunk scent glands were not the kind of small talk you wanted your dad to whip out while your friends were over—*so embarrassing!*

"Short for call-up-a-storm. That's what people used to call loons—they thought their cries brought in the storm clouds. Isn't that neat?" her dad asked.

"Super neat," Bee muttered, watching the dark patches between the long, stoic pines for wildlife as they drove by.

"This is way better than some amusement park in . . . in . . ." Mr. Bakshi frowned. "Where was it Kitty's folks were going, again?"

"Florida," Bee said.

"Oh my, that sounds nice," Granny squeaked. "What's in Florida? Are we going there, too?"

"Definitely not," Bee muttered softly, turning away from the window and crossing her arms.

Kitty and Bee had been looking forward to the grand opening of the Betsy Chillers amusement park for months, but not just because they wanted to ride the Ferris Wheel of Impending Doom, or the Roller Coaster of Ghosts You Can Never Unsee, or the Try-It-If-You-Dare Scream Drop of Death.

Kitty and Bee were *true fans*, you see.

They'd read all forty-two Betsy Chillers books as they came out (Bee had to read Kitty's copies, of course—her parents refused to buy them), started an after-school Betsy Chillers club dedicated to the study of all things spooky (the two of them ate gummy worms and rewatched their favorite moments from the Betsy Chillers movies), and stayed up way too late so they wouldn't miss out on the limited edition online release of the accompanying *Betsy Chillers Field Guide to the Paranormal.* In short, Betsy Chillers—with her loopy dark locks and billowing white blouse and sharp-as-a-knife grin—was their monster-butt-kicking hero.

The day Bee found out Kitty's parents wanted to bring her on their Florida trip to visit the Betsy Chillers amusement park for the exclusive early release of book forty-three was the best day of her life. The worst day of her life was when her parents announced they were going on a family cottage trip instead. And it was non-negotiable.

"If you ask me, those books are much too scary." Her mom shook her head as the car took another sharp turn. "Some time away from all that creepiness will do you some good."

Bee felt her ears warm. "Everyone's reading them; they're written for *kids*. Plus, the stories are really good! Betsy kicks some serious monster butt, and there's always a mystery to solve, too. *You* read mysteries, Mom!"

But Mom just clicked her tongue against her teeth. "Trust me, those Betsy Chillers are no mysteries. And they're much too scary for you."

Bee gritted her teeth with frustration, then sighed, her heart sinking into the hollow of her stomach. It was on ongoing battle with her parents. Betsy Chillers was too scary, piles of garbage were treasures waiting to be discovered, and her friends would always leave her house with a wildlife factoid they didn't ask for. Unlike Kitty's parents, Bee's just didn't get it. And they never would.

"STOP THE CAR!" her mom suddenly cried.

The cooler and the pillows and Granny lurched forward as the car came to a stop at a fork in the road. To the left, the trees swayed darker, with more pines and cedars blocking out the light. To the right, glimpses of blue from the lake blinked in between pockets of low bramble and raspberry bushes. In the center of the fork rested a sun-bleached trailer that looked like it had been there for a hundred years. The remains of a gravel driveway were littered with tufts of grass and dead leaves, the only space on the property that wasn't completely taken back by the forest.

11

And near the road, next to a small garbage bag, lay an old, rusted bike.

From either side of the car, the whine of mosquitoes slowly found its way to Bee.

"Doesn't it look like a perfectly good bike?" Bee's mom flashed a smile. "Once we fix it up, you can ride around while we're at the cottage! I'm going to ask the owners if we can take it."

Bee squinted at the tangle of bike chain and twisted spokes, with remnants of glittery streamers wrapped around the handlebars. Even though it had succumbed to the rust of what looked like many, many winters, flecks of the original brown remained, and here and there she spotted a touch of pink. In short, it had to be the ugliest bike she'd ever seen. But for some strange reason, she couldn't tear her eyes away from it. Her pulse slowed to a dull thud, and for a moment, her mom's voice blurred into the background.

Bee wasn't one to get spooked easily. When Betsy Chillers was about to face the two-headed monster with the power to smother all light, and the lamp in Bee's bedroom suddenly flickered, she didn't even wince. When Betsy Chillers found herself trapped in a cave of spirits, about to get possessed, and at the exact same moment Bee was flooded with an unexplainable coldness that sank right to her bones, she barely batted an eyelash. They were coincidences, otherwise known as the loose electrical wiring of an older house and a very drafty window.

But she felt it now, staring at the old bike: an itchiness climbing up her throat, daring her to scream, and a buzzing in her ear whispering *stay away*. And she couldn't explain it.

Or maybe the humid air combined with her embarrassing parents was finally getting to her. Bee's hand came down hard against her forearm, reducing a pesky bug into a bloody smudge that stained the braided bracelet tied snugly around her wrist. She shook her head.

"Please don't ask anyone, Mom," she begged. "I don't want to ride that thing. Anyways, there's no one around."

"Nonsense, with a little fixing up we can give this bike a new home." Bee's mom stuck her head out the window, her gold bangles clinking madly as she waved an arm toward the abandoned trailer. "Hello there!" she called out.

"What are you doing? There's no one—" Bee stopped as a dark beige patch she'd mistaken for rust detached itself from a folding canvas lawn chair and hobbled over. The lady was long and sinewy, with a squat head that strongly resembled a toad's, and a shaggy brown overcoat that looked permanently wet. *And what's with that mole above her eye, sprouting some kind of white fungus? And the shag of brown swaying around her face like branches?* Bee flinched as a large reddish beetle landed on the woman's shoulder, nearly blending in.

"And you thought you wouldn't get spooked this

week," Bee's dad joked, and then scowled as her mom slyly jabbed his side.

"Excuse me, we're the Bakshis!" she said in her warmest, cheeriest, friendliest tone. "We're staying at our friends' cottage for the week. Are you getting rid of this bike?"

The lady stopped a few feet away from the car and tilted her chin out; one eye pointed left and the other right, just like the forked road. The beetle scuttled into the mess of her hair.

"Not from around here, are ya?" Her voice carried to them like rustling leaves, low and raspy and a little bit dead.

Bee's mom paused, and Bee seriously considered ducking below the car window. A brown family in a beat-up car asking if they could take someone else's junk? Could it be any clearer they didn't belong? *Sooo embarrassing!*

The lady tilted her chin again, then spat to one side.

"Oh yes, that's right," Mrs. Bakshi exclaimed, plastering her smile back on. "We're only renting out—"

"You can have it," the lady interrupted.

Bee watched with disgust as the beetle moved to the woman's eyebrow, and then onto her *eye*. The lady didn't flinch; she didn't even seem to notice. Then the eye swiveled wildly, staring right at Bee. The woman mouthed something, but it wasn't quite loud enough, and Bee couldn't be sure of the words, exactly. She ducked, neck burning as she slid low into her seat.

A chill ran down her spine.

"Would you mind putting it aside? We'll come back for it! Thank you!" Bee's mom called out above the crunch of the gravel as they rolled away.

She pulled herself back into the car and Bee let out a sigh of relief as the strange feeling that had gripped her at the sight of the beetle-eyed lady and the old bike crumbled away.

"Well, she seemed lovely," Mrs. Bakshi said. "Oh, and there's the new neighbors! The Joneses!"

Bee ventured a peek out the window as they passed the well-kept lawn and back deck of a recently reno-vated cottage. A girl with long dark hair and a billowing white pirate's blouse sat with one leg on the deck railing and the other dangling into space. The girl lifted her head as they passed, but didn't wave. Bee couldn't tell from a distance, but she looked about her own age.

She frowned. There was something . . . familiar about her.

"I heard they recently bought the place," her mom continued. "We should introduce ourselves later! It would be nice to make them feel welcomed."

Bee grimaced. "More like weird. We're only here for like, a week, remember? We don't actually live here— we don't even own a cottage."

The car crunched to a stop and Bee stepped outside.

"One day you're going to realize that we're not weird

15

at all," her dad said as he turned off the engine. "We're cool, Binita. Repeat after me—*kewl*."

Granny, who at some point had fallen asleep, woke up with a start. "What? What did you say?" she asked. "Are we here?"

"Binita, darling, please help unload the car, would you?" her mom asked.

Bee sighed as she checked her phone one last time. There was an old video message from earlier that day, frozen on a picture of Kitty with her lips pursed and pointing at what looked like a spooky merry-go-round. Her blond hair was parted into two French braids and lay silky and flat over a brand-new halter top. Bee touched the play icon, but the picture remained frozen. *No Wi-Fi. Great.* The eerie sound of a loon's cry echoed off the lake like a ghostly howl.

"You know," Bee's dad said, raising his bushy eyebrows, "the loon's call has even been described as a warning."

"A warning for what?" Bee asked, gently linking arms with Granny as they walked toward the cottage.

"A warning that danger is coming."

Bee rolled her eyes. *Danger of boredom, maybe.*

· 2 ·

Dark Waters
and Stinky Marshes

Bee was used to going camping—there had been more than a few family backcountry camping trips over the years and more than her fair share of horseflies—but this was her first time at a cottage. The Gladers' cottage, to be precise.

The Gladers were old family friends of Granny's. They had taken the approach of slowly expanding their cottage into a jumble of different buildings all smooshed on top of each other. A log living room add-on here. An extra bedroom made of brick there. A second stone well, because why not? Bee's gaze zeroed in on the large trampoline peeking out from the side of the house. But the best part had to be the lake view.

She slipped off her sandals and stepped barefoot

onto the graying planks of the floating dock, putting one foot in front of the other and watching the small ripples dance away. It was a smallish lake, surrounded by thick forest and brownish cattails that camouflaged the neighbors on either side. But from the edge of the dock, Bee could see more—a handful of other docks poking out from the tree line, glimpses of thatched roofs and flower beds between the pines, and the pale forms of people tanning facedown, looking a bit like the zombies from *Betsy Chillers: March of the Undead*.

There was a lot of creepy in the world, once you started to look. She leaned out over the edge of the dock, watching as a water spider skimmed over her reflection, and frowned at the memory of the beetle-eyed lady and the old bike. Betsy Chillers's first rule of thumb: Never dismiss a chill.

The eerie cry of a loon sounded again, making Bee jump.

"Yeehaw!"

Mr. Bakshi's yowl reverberated across the lake, followed closely by the thunder of footsteps crashing down the dock. He bounded past Bee in his fuchsia shorts and careened into the water. A sizable amount of lake water rocketed into the air and splashed back toward Bee.

"Daaad," she whined, cringing as the cold soaked into her capris and wishing very hard that not too many people had witnessed his spectacular entrance. Kitty's dad never acted like this.

Luckily, the tanning zombies didn't budge.

Her dad surfaced like a creature from the deep, algae speckling his tall forehead and goggles suctioned onto his eye sockets.

"Did you know Canada has more lakes than the rest of the world combined?" he sang, floating on his back and beaming at the sky. "Come take advantage of it! Come in!"

Bee's dad was the kind of person who always wore his bathing shorts under his pants during the summer months, just in case the opportunity for a swim presented itself. And now that cringeworthy opportunity had finally arrived.

"Go with your father," Bee's mom called.

Oh great, everyone's here now.

Her mother, dressed in a flowery pink one-piece, and Granny, wrapped in a neon-orange sarong, made their way down the yard's gentle slope toward a lone plastic chair waiting on the sand. After Granny settled into it, Bee's mom marched to the dock and, with a flick of the wrist, unfurled a yoga mat (*where did she get that from?!*). As it happened, Mrs. Bakshi felt the same way about impromptu stretching opportunities as Mr. Bakshi did about swimming.

Well, if the neighbors didn't notice us before, they will now.

"You know I don't like lake water," Bee said, trying to make her voice small to compensate for the chaos of her family. "And what about the deadly blue algae dad was going on about? Are we *sure* it's all gone?"

Truth be told, it wasn't the algae that concerned her.

"Pff! He was exaggerating earlier, but take the canoe if it bothers you." Her mom pointed to a glint of metal in the bushes by the beach.

Her dad floated lazily past, bringing his arms up and over his head in an easy backstroke.

"Just go across the lake and back," she encouraged. "I'll be watching from here."

Bee nodded, tugging the canoe free and floating it to the end of the dock. Anything to get a break from the family. Or to make sure the neighbors didn't see them.

Carefully, she stepped inside, shuffled into a damp life jacket, and settled on the cold, hard bench seat. It wasn't that Bee didn't know how to swim. Quite the opposite. Her parents were firm believers in swimming as a life skill, and on top of weekly Saturday swimming lessons, most of her Sundays were spent at the local pool, where a minimum of ten laps were required before she was allowed to play (them were the rules). But lake water . . . It was the unknown of what lay underneath, waiting— all the scaly and squirmy and fishy things she couldn't see. Bee shivered. Lake water was a different beast.

She dipped the paddle below the dark surface, urging

the canoe forward. It took a few strokes to get going, it took a bit of muscle, but soon the boat sliced through the water effortlessly.

She paused as she reached the center of the lake. As the canoe came to a standstill, it angled slightly, giving her a sideways view of the next-door neighbors' cottage, where she had seen the pirate-dressed girl. It had strong lines and a tall A-frame fitted with wide windows. Their dock was surprisingly close by, separated from the Gladers' property by only a thin line of tall cattails where a bright red canoe was resting. There was no sign of its inhabitants, though.

Bee squinted as she glanced back. *Oh my gosh.* The Gladers' dock was very visible from there, with Mrs. Bakshi in a full downward dog. Bee dipped the paddle back in, pulling forward hard to escape the embarrassing sight.

Whereas most of the lake's border was well-kept, with sandy beaches, docks, segments of overhanging cedar, and pockets of cattails, the far side of the lake was pierced from beneath by the long white limbs of bleached tree trunks and branches.

"Ew, what's that smell?" Bee brought the paddle across her knees and let the canoe drift forward.

Several painted turtles slipped off their smooth perches and into the water at her approach. Then a patch of water next to the canoe shuddered and Bee peered over the edge cautiously. Her fingers trembled ever so slightly and there was a tightness in her throat. *What was that?* Dark curls rose up like gnarled seaweed, followed by the glint of a dark wrinkly forehead and bushy eyebrows.

"Boo!" Bee's dad grinned, keeping his head above water. "Did I get you?"

"Dad!" she whined, grabbing hold of her seat.

"I think that's close enough to the shore," he said, moving his goggles to his forehead.

As her breath and the canoe steadied themselves, Bee gazed past the dead trees and cedar coverage to the forest beyond, ignoring the cloud of small swamp flies forming around her hair. It looked like a neglected lot, but better. *A creepy neglected lot.*

Pine needles and branches covered the ground, and a barely visible cobblestone walkway led up into the woods. What could have been a wide, beautiful beach instead steamed with the deep earthy pungency of stagnant water and marsh.

"Abandoned for decades, after a terrible fire burned it down." Bee's dad shook his head. "Apparently it was some kids' prank. Too bad. Looks like it could be a nice spot."

The wind whistled over the lake, pushing away the flies and making the branches wave from the shore.

Bee tilted her head. Between the marsh stink and the fresh pine, there was something else on the air.

Something sweet and pleasant and warm, with the faintest hint of spice. Something that Bee couldn't quite place, and that certainly didn't belong wafting from an abandoned lot. But then it was gone, and her dad was smacking his goggles back on and diving underwater.

"I'm coming," Bee muttered, half to her dad but mostly to herself.

There was something about that abandoned lot. Something about it that Betsy Chillers wouldn't ignore. A small smile tickled the corner of her lips. It seemed as though her family's week at the cottage just got a little less boring.

The paddle swooshed as she carved a reverse stroke through the water, swinging the bow back toward the cottage. Bee waited, tense, as the small rocking she had caused subsided, before plunging the paddle back in.

The water glistened darkly as a shadow passed underneath. *Not again.*

"Dad, stop it. I know it's you." Bee rolled her eyes, then frowned. Her dad had surfaced up ahead, nowhere near the canoe. His arms came up every few seconds in a perfect crawl, and a mound of bubbles rose in his wake.

Bee froze. Her heart drummed and her forehead prickled. *It could have been a turtle,* she reasoned. *There were so many on the logs earlier. Right?* She let go of her breath, watching intently for any odd ripple or wave. But whatever secrets the lake held, they stayed hidden beneath the surface. For now.

· 3 ·

An Annoying Encounter

Usually when camping out in a tent, Bee found it was difficult to sleep in past six in the morning. First the chickadees and the chipmunks and the sparrows started twitting and chirping from the treetops and the firepit. Then it was the beaming rays of sunlight, bursting through the tent netting directly into the eyeballs. And lastly, the long solo call of the loon, reverberating over the lake as the mist evaporated.

But Bee didn't hear any of that, because she wasn't camping in a tent: she was cottaging. The birds had already sung their morning chorus and the lake was clear and mist-free by the time she dragged herself out from the single bed and into the living room.

24

"What is *that*?" She rubbed her eyes, staring at the large bronze Kali statue perched on the living room side table. "Why did you bring it from home?"

It was a familiar statue, with the goddess of doomsday, Kali, standing on the goddess Shiva, long hair flowing down her back and a necklace of heads against her chest—to show that even the darkness of death had its place in nature.

"I didn't bring it from home, I bought it," her mom said happily.

She stood over a sizzling cast-iron pan in the kitchen, decked in snazzy striped yoga pants and an embroidered Kerala tunic.

Mom actually bought something? For full price?

"I picked it up at that secondhand store. You know, the one Granny told us about."

At the mention of her name, Granny smiled widely from the kitchen table before returning her gaze to the window to observe the view. Well, "observe" was a strong word. Granny was mostly blind but could still see light and movement. To Granny's eyes, Bee expected the large front window appeared like a square of sunshine in an otherwise dim room.

"It's a gift for the Gladers, for lending us their cottage," Mrs. Bakshi continued.

Bee grimaced but kept her thoughts to herself. *Even our gifts are weird! But at least I won't be around when they get it.* She made her way to the table, strewn with dirty dishes. It looked like everyone else had already eaten.

"Where's Dad?" Bee asked, stacking the dishes quickly and making a clean area for herself. But before her butt touched the chair, Granny reached out a shaky hand.

"Could you fetch me a glass of water?" she asked. "I'm parched."

Bee sighed, standing back up.

The tantalizing scent of fried egg on paratha reached her nose as she moved through the kitchen, taking care to avoid her mom in the tight space.

"He's gone to get that bike and borrow some tools to fix it up," Bee's mom explained, plating the paratha. "Did you want to ask him something?"

Right, the bike. Bee swallowed the beginnings of an unexplainable itchiness at the back of her throat. If the abandoned lot was calling her closer like a sweet pot of freshly brewed chai, the bike was its opposite—a rusted death trap covered in sparkly streamers. There was no way she was getting anywhere near that thing.

She *had* wanted to ask her dad whether she could take the canoe out by herself and explore (because he was the most likely parent to agree), but maybe her mom would do. Bee would just have to leave out a few choice details on her destination.

There was something about the abandoned lot. The

dead tree limbs tangled around the shore as though to keep people out, the thick wall of cedars, and that oddly sweet aroma that swept through the stink of the marsh . . . It wasn't the grand opening of the Betsy Chillers amusement park. But it might still be spooky enough to make for a good story to share with Kitty later.

"Mom . . . ," Bee started hesitantly. "I was thinking . . . wondering, actually . . . could I go and explore on my own today?"

Mrs. Bakshi swept by to collect the dishes. "Explore? Where will you be exploring, exactly?" She raised her eyebrows suspiciously.

It was difficult to get anything past her, especially mischief.

"The lake?" Bee asked tentatively.

Bee's mom turned her back to the kitchen table as she hunched over the sink, gears turning (she was also skilled in the wizardry of saying no without saying no).

"Sure, Binita, you can do your exploring," she said, plunging the dishes into the soapy sink water. "But first please go for a walk. It's good exercise."

Bee turned to Granny, whose head had bobbed back onto her chest and flowery beige lapel for a power nap.

"All right," Bee said. "And then afterwards I can go explore?"

"As long as you have time to help me prepare the food for tonight," she said evenly. "I'm having the neighbors over for supper!"

Oh great. If there was one thing Bee could count on with her folks, it was that there was always a dinner party around the corner. And if you'd just had one, then another was on its way. Her mom always said it was part of their culture to be welcoming and hospitable and always ready with a cup of tea to offer. Which to Bee just meant there were more opportunities to be totally and utterly mortified.

"Fiiine," she sighed.

The air was still slightly crisp from the evening before, but judging by the strength of the sun streaming through the leaves overhead, it was going to be another hot day.

"Lovely morning," Granny commented.

With her large pink sun hat and even larger sunglasses, she looked like she belonged on the set of a classic horror film—you know, the black-and-white ones from the golden age of monster movies. But somehow, she always pulled it off.

"Yes, it is," Bee said, letting her fingers graze the trunk of one of the many pines.

The smell of their recently applied mosquito repellent followed them as they shuffled up the driveway to the cottage-country gravel road (Granny only had one speed, and that was s-l-o-w).

Which way, which way. What Bee was really thinking was which way were they likely to meet the fewest number of people? The Gladers' cottage was one of the first along the path, so it stood to reason that the best way forward was to the right, the way they had driven in. At most there would be only two cottages to pass by—the new neighbors and the scary lady who lived in the trailer—and at best they would bump into no one. Straight ahead was a thin dirt trail leading away from the main road, but it was much too narrow for Granny.

I'll have to come back and explore the trail later, Bee mused.

The wavery thrum of Granny's humming mixed with the *crunch, crunch* of the gravel underfoot. It felt nice, familiar.

Granny often picked Bee up after swimming lessons, and they would walk arm in arm, singing and humming. Bee used to look forward to those walks, which sometimes seemed endless, especially when Granny started forgetting things like which street to turn down. She frowned, recalling Kitty's smile when she met Granny for the first time, before she'd leaned in close to Bee so no one else could hear and whispered, "Does your grandma have to hum all the time? It's a bit . . . weird."

"Do you have to sing, Granny?" Bee asked.

"The birds are singing, aren't they?" Granny said, pausing her questionable rendition of "Singin' in the Rain." "And it's good to make noise when you're in the woods. Keeps the witches and bears at bay."

Bee couldn't help but grin. Granny would probably fit right in with her after-school Betsy Chillers club.

Unfortunately, the grin didn't last long.

"Hi there!" someone yelled.

Bee looked up reluctantly at the boy hanging from the neighbor's back porch, his bike leaning against the railing. She smiled and waved without stopping, as the bare minimum of common courtesy required.

"Hey, wait up!" he called.

Bee cringed and turned as the boy bounded from the porch and raced to meet them. He was around the same height as her, but the mess of curly red hair piled high above his freckled face must have given him an extra five inches, at least. And it wasn't just any shade of red—this was a blazing, fire-truck, you-couldn't-not-notice-me-if-you-wanted type of red hair. But that wasn't the issue.

Suctioned to his eyes below his red eyebrows and constellation of freckles was a pair of blue swimming goggles. And there was no other sign that he was about to go swimming.

He extended a hand eagerly, and then when Bee waited a second too long to react, grasped her hand anyway, shaking vigorously.

"Hi! I'm Lucas. And your mom came by earlier and dropped off these weird pancake things." He brought his other hand up, showcasing a cold, folded paratha, and then ripped a large bite out of it. "Yummy, though!"

"Good morning, young man." Granny smiled in his

general direction before breaking back into humming.

Bee adjusted her glasses, unable to take her eyes off the goggles. She swept her frizzy curls behind her ears.

"We have them all the time for breakfast. I'm Bee." She gestured to her own face. "What's with the goggles?" *Why would anyone wear those if they weren't going swimming? For fun?*

Lucas raised his eyebrows. "My ghost specs! They help me see things that others can't." He ripped off another large mouthful of paratha. "There's a lot of creepy in the world, once you start to look."

"That's what I always say!" Bee blurted out. She couldn't believe it—twelve-year-old fans of the bizarre and creepy were few and far between.

Lucas nodded excitedly. "Like the other day, I was brushing my teeth, and when I checked the mirror, I swear I saw a real ghost! I mean, I think it was a ghost. Could have been steam from the shower . . ."

"Wait." Her smile faded. "You actually believe it's real?"

"You don't?" Lucas asked. He twitched his nose, making the goggles wiggle around. "You know what, it's all right. Everyone has their own thing, so I promise not to hold it against you." He smiled. "Friends?"

On second thought, he was a bit odd. The kind of odd that Kitty would never let join the Betsy Chillers club. Bee's ears warmed from secondhand embarrassment. Because it seemed this kid was immune to feeling

31

embarrassed for himself.

She glanced past him at the large back porch and the cottage beyond, where the girl with the long dark hair and the billowing white pirate's blouse had been. *That must be his sister. She seemed pretty cool.*

Lucas wiped his face with the back of his hand, which did nothing for the flakes and crumbs of paratha that clung resolutely to his mouth.

Then again, anyone would seem cooler than this kid.

No, she couldn't be friends with Lucas. Even though she wanted to. Bee sighed, composing herself.

"I already have a friend. Kitty. I was *going* to spend this week with her at this amusement park in Florida. But instead I'm here with my family." Bee did her best to stick to the facts. "We're renting the cottage for the week only. So technically we're not really neighbors."

The edges of Lucas's lips curled downward, and the eager light in his expression dimmed.

"Oh," he said, adjusting his goggles. "All right, then."

Bee's chest tightened a bit as he sauntered off back to his porch, but she pushed the feeling away. Staying under the radar with a weird kid like Lucas would be downright impossible, and she already had enough problems. Maybe Bee had ultra-embarrassing parents for whom getting a thank-you gift meant visiting the secondhand shop for a South Asian death god, but at least she *tried* to fit in. Unlike Lucas, who seemed to be trying extra hard to stick out.

But even as she continued along the gravel path, Granny humming and the birds singing in the background, she couldn't help but wonder. Maybe Lucas knew something about the lady with the bug on her eye? Maybe he knew something about the abandoned lot across the lake? After all, one ghost-believing goggle-wearing friend was certainly better than none. As long as Kitty never found out, that is.

· 4 ·

Feast of Starlight

Bee certainly meant to take the canoe out the moment she returned to the cottage. In fact, she was surveying the lake from the deck that wrapped around the back of the cottage, trying to determine if those kayaks over there were coming closer or moving farther away, when the screen door creaked and Granny stumbled out, requiring an immediate helping hand.

"Thank you, dear," she said as Bee lowered her into one of the deck's four red Adirondack chairs. "What a life we lead, huh? What a life!"

"Yes, it's nice here, isn't it," Bee agreed hurriedly. Not that she didn't enjoy spending time with Granny, but she did have places to explore and secrets to uncover.

Betsy Chillers's second rule of thumb: When you have a hunch, follow it.

Bee jumped down the porch steps before Granny could ask for any favors, ready to race down the grassy slope to the water. Unfortunately, at that exact moment, her parents waltzed around the corner, back from their hike.

"We're going to need as many dry twigs as you can find," her dad said, pointing to the undergrowth near the property's edge. "They're perfect fire starters if we want a nice fire tonight. And it will be good to clean up a bit for the Gladers."

Bee eyed the large trampoline and then the outdoor firepit beside it, lined with large lake rocks and a few log stumps. The smoky, burned smell of roasted marshmallows from past camping trips filled her nostrils, and she held back a sigh of exasperation. Was everyone against her getting to the lake today?

She wandered near the edge of the water, collecting dead branches and swatting at rogue mosquitoes. A little way past the dock, something white and glistening caught her eye. Bee crouched between the lakeside boulders, using a stick to poke at what looked like the remains of some rodent. Two long teeth poked out of its skull, while maggots wriggled through what was left of the decomposing carcass. *Cool.*

By the time Bee looked back toward the lake and the glint of the metal canoe, it was already afternoon, which meant helping her mom start dinner preparations.

She entered the kitchen through the screen door, dragging her feet and preparing to put up a half-hearted protest. Already the aroma of fried ginger and onion and garlic (or as Granny liked to say, the holy trinity of ingredients in any Indian dish) permeated the cottage.

"Did you have a nice time exploring, Binita?" her mom asked, adding a handful of spices to the oily sizzle.

Bay leaf, cardamom, cumin, turmeric, garam masala. The wonderful aroma was nearly enough to put Bee's unsuccessful morning of exploration behind her.

"Oh, did you go exploring?" her dad exclaimed from the table, standing over a pile of atta flour. "Find anything interesting? Remember, lots of poisonous mushrooms look a lot like the kind we eat, so if you see a mushroom, leave it be."

The soft whistle of Granny taking her afternoon nap glided in from the back bedroom. The radio was tuned to her parents' favorite international station, and a slow rendition of the Gipsy Kings' top hits strummed in the background.

Because we can't be like everyone else and listen to pop or soft rock or something . . .

"Will the neighbors be into this kind of . . . food?" Bee asked nervously, watching as her father created a small hole in the center of his flour and poured in warm water.

Gently, gently, he folded the flour into the water,

kneading it into a ball of dough. Bee walked over, sinking her finger into the glutinous bouncy goodness. Granny used to be in charge of the chapatis. She remembered her sectioning off pieces and rolling them out into palm-size rounds. Once they were toasted on the stove, it had been Bee's job to place a small nugget of ghee between each finished chapati to ensure they didn't stick.

"I'm sure Lucas and his mom, Hanna, have had Indian before," Bee's mom said as she added washed lentils to the pot. The sizzling instantly died down. "And everyone enjoys delicious food."

Crinkles formed between Bee's eyebrows as she eyed the Kali statue.

"What about Lucas's sister? Isn't she coming?"

"I didn't realize he had a sister, but I would assume so! Now, why don't you change into something brighter." Her mom raised her thin eyebrows. "What about that new shirt you got from your cousin?"

"You mean the new hand-me-down?" A frilly orange shirt that Bee had definitely left at home on purpose. "It doesn't even look like it's from this decade."

"No worries," her mom said calmly, ignoring the completely valid complaint. "I packed it for you."

Bee huffed. Kitty's parents never made her wear her cousins' old clothes. And Kitty would *never* wear this.

"Don't be ungrateful, Binita—it's a nice top!" Bee's mom tapped the side of her curry pot with the ladle.

"Granny reminded me of that many times growing up. There's more to life than having the latest brand-name clothes. And now I'm reminding you."

Bee did not change her shirt. Instead, as the lentils simmered and the coconut rice bubbled, she found herself floating toward the couch and flipping through an old nature magazine to an article on loons. She ran a finger over the glossy close-up of its deep red eyes. Blood red.

"Can hold their breath underwater for up to five minutes while fishing." Hmm, that might explain the thing under the water yesterday.

The screen door creaked and Bee jumped up, the magazine slipping off her chest and onto the ground. Through the window, the setting sun cast shimmering pinks and oranges across the lake like an ocean of fire.

"Hello, Hanna! Lucas! Come in, come in," her mom said, putting the curry back on the heat (curries tasted better when made in advance—the longer they sat, the deeper the flavor).

Lucas bobbed forward, making room for Hanna in the doorway. Unlike her son's fiery locks, she had light brown braids that hung limply above her shoulders.

There was no one else. Bee's shoulders slumped in disappointment. Maybe Lucas's sister had already caught on that Bee's family was weird and decided not to come.

"I brought some dessert," Hanna said, her voice as

soft as her milky features, handing Bee's mom a large plate.

A gingerbread house. The warm scent curled around Bee like tendrils, and for some reason, she couldn't tear her gaze away. It was so intricate, the roof tiled with brown icing and black jelly beans, the window-sills lined with chocolate chips carved into the shape of flowerpots. There even seemed to be a shadow behind the chocolate-bark door, as though someone was peering through the melted-sugar glass. . . . Bee's breathing quickened as the light around her dimmed. Something wasn't right.

The gingerbread house shuddered and Bee gasped. *Is anyone else seeing this?* But if they did, the adults didn't react, continuing their exchange of pleasantries as a few jelly beans tumbled off the roof and the chocolate-bark door creaked and stretched.

And then, in an explosion of icing and cinnamon, the whole candy house began to grow, the walls climbing and the bricks expanding. Hanna dropped it to the floor as it overtook her, blocking out the dining table and her parents and Lucas. But still it grew, pushing against the roof of the cottage.

"Mom? Dad?" Bee called out to them, but no one responded. She turned around and froze.

She wasn't in the cottage anymore. The stars winked above her and the wind howled as she stared at the towering gingerbread house. Her heart was beating so fast, she could hardly hear the loons crying over the lake. And then the shadow lurking behind the chocolate-bark door moved.

The screen door creaked and Bee startled awake, throwing the magazine to the ground. A bead of sweat dripped from her forehead as she pushed herself up. *Just a dream. It was just a dream.*

"Hello, Hanna! Lucas! Come in!" her mom said, putting the curry back on the heat.

Lucas and Hanna hurried inside, closing the screen door quickly behind them so as not to let in any mosquitoes.

There was a tenseness in Bee's shoulders and a lump in her throat. She'd never met Lucas's mom before, and yet she looked exactly the same as the Hanna from her dream, with the addition of a dried rose stuck above her ear and fastened with a crisscross of bobby pins. Hopefully the similarities ended there.

"I brought something sweet," Hanna said.

Bee froze, holding her breath.

"Iced tea! Delicious, thank you!" Bee's mom grasped the pitcher of sloshing brown liquid, and Bee breathed a sigh of relief.

Thank goodness.

Suddenly aware of her own state (the bed head was particularly bad), Bee rolled off the couch and onto the floor, scuttling unseen into the bathroom. She roughly brushed her fingers through her hair and pulled it back into a low pony, listening to the adults' chatter.

"We decided to leave Al at home—she wasn't feeling well," Hanna explained as dishes clattered, a sure sign that her dad was setting the table.

"Poor Al, we'll have to meet her next time," her mom said. "I know Bee was looking forward to playing with her."

Bee's neck warmed. Why were parents always doing that? Talking about their kids when they thought they weren't listening?

"Aw, that's sweet. Lucas is the same," she heard Hanna answer. "They get along so well."

Bee hovered in front of the mirror for a bit longer, her pulse suddenly quick. Would they find her dad too loud and his nature facts too annoying? Would her mom start talking about her favorite secondhand store and how she got such a good deal buying her spices in bulk? Would the neighbors enjoy her family's cooking? She recalled the first time Kitty came over after school, how she'd pinched her nose when the spices began to sizzle in the kitchen. *It smells different.*

"Binitaaa!"

Mrs. Bakshi's call found its way to Bee's ear, shaking her out of her thoughts. The sound of chairs being pulled back. Cutlery clinking.

"Maybe she went outside?" her dad suggested.

"I'm here, sorry." Bee opened the bathroom door,

stalking forward and avoiding everyone's eyes. "Nice to meet you."

Everyone else was already seated, with an empty chair waiting between Granny and Lucas. He tore his goggled eyes from the coconut rice at her approach, his polo shirt tucked into the elastic waistband of his shorts in a semblance of dress attire.

"Hi, Bee!" he said, his smile wavering only slightly when she kept her lips pressed shut.

"So nice to meet you," Hanna said softly, tucking her hair behind the rose. "And thank you again for having us. This all looks incredibly delicious!"

The spread was impressive: the vibrant yellow of egg curry dotted with the snow-white of hard-boiled eggs, the fluffy coconut rice laced with saffron, the pile of steaming chapatis glistening with ghee . . . Mouth watering, Bee waited patiently to serve herself (guests and elders were always served first), but just as the bowls finally reached her, Granny gave a small cough.

"I'm feeling a bit parched," she said, leaning toward Bee.

Bee put the serving spoon back down. "Don't worry, I'll get you some water," she said quietly.

Conversation flowed easily between Hanna and the Bakshis. Apparently, Lucas and his mom planned to live at the cottage year-round since Lucas's father had recently passed away.

"Homeschooling was a good option for us," Hanna

said, taking a sip of iced tea. "What with my sister living in the area, me working from home as a writer, and Lucas having so much trouble at school . . ."

"*Mo-om*," Lucas complained, his face turning a deep shade of purple.

Hanna patted his hand. "Sorry, hon, sorry. It's just so difficult for kids to make friends these days, I find."

"Oh, definitely." Bee's dad nodded. "But all you need is one good friend. It makes all the difference. Right, Bee?"

"*I* don't have trouble at school," Bee muttered, glancing at Lucas.

But the conversation had already moved on to Hanna's interest in dried flowers and ventures into herb growing. And it kept going on and on (grown-ups never seemed to run out of things to talk about) until the sun dipped below the tree line and the stars came out and the moon traced a silver-white crescent on the dark waters and Granny's chin dipped onto her chest. And somehow, everyone seemed to get along fine.

"Excuse me just a moment." Bee's mom got up, wiping tears of laughter from her eyes. "I need to use the loo."

Bee turned to her father as he began to clear the table. "Aren't we going to have a fire and roast marshmallows?"

She'd been patient and quiet all this time—dessert was a necessity. Even Lucas perked up.

Her dad passed a hand over his high hairline. "I don't think so. Maybe tomorrow night."

Bee huffed.

"But I have a better idea," he said. "There's supposed to be a meteor shower starting tonight—the ultimate light show! If you go lie out on the trampoline, you might spot a few earlier ones. Wouldn't that be special?"

Lying outside on a trampoline with Lucas? Watching a meteor shower? It all seemed a bit much for someone she just met.

But before Bee could counter, Lucas was out of his chair.

"Meteor shower? Like shooting stars? That's so cool!" He looked at Bee expectantly.

"Fine, we'll go." Bee sighed, grabbing a hoodie from the couch and the bug repellent from the entrance table.

The air was cold, as it usually was once the sun disappeared in the late summer months, taking its warmth with it. Bee nestled deeper into her hoodie. The trampoline's tight netting was damp to the touch as she lay down, taking care to keep a wide berth between herself and Lucas.

"There are so many stars here," he said, settling into corpse pose (the very real name of a yoga position) and tucking the throw blanket Mr. Bakshi had insisted they bring outside up to his chin.

"Did you know some animals, like ducks, use stars to navigate?" Bee asked, then pursed her lips, embarrassed. *I'm turning into my dad with these facts!* She could see Kitty now, rolling her eyes.

Bee waited for the inevitable remarks. *What was that funny-looking statue?* and *Why does your grandma randomly start humming?* and *Why are your clothes so . . . old-looking?* But Lucas remained quiet, and the stars blinked in a still sky, and there were no shooting stars to be seen.

"My granny has this thing called dementia," Bee continued, feeling the sudden urge to explain herself. "And my mom's family moved to Canada when she was a kid. We're pretty much a normal family. We go camping sometimes, my dad's going to school at some university, my mom works at a library . . ."

"Granny?" Lucas asked quietly before sinking back into silence.

Bee waved her hand by her ears, shooing away the determined mosquitoes. This was exactly why she didn't want her family to invite people over. This was exactly the kind of thing she wanted to avoid.

He thinks we're weirdos. He definitely thinks we're weirdos. Bee stewed in her feelings, until finally, she couldn't take it a second longer and was strongly considering going back inside.

"You said you didn't want to be friends," Lucas said, his voice small.

The hot air in Bee's belly deflated, and she remembered what his mom had said at the dinner table. *Right.*

I did say that, didn't I. . . .

"It's not that I don't *want* to be your friend," Bee explained, trying to find the right words. "I didn't even want to come here in the first place. My family just doesn't fit in here—they don't even try. And then people start looking, and the more people look, the more I . . ."

Bee's chest tightened. She had enough trouble trying to appear normal as it was. The last thing she needed was to hang out with the weird kid at the cottage. She grimaced, taking in his eager eyes and beaming, crumb-dusted smile. *I should let him down easy.*

"I don't want to give my parents an excuse to come back here again next summer," she said, a little too quickly. "That's why we can't be friends." It wasn't a full lie. But it wasn't a full truth, either.

A pause, as Lucas digested her explanation.

"Oh, I get it," he said, and Bee could almost hear him smiling. "You don't want your folks to know you're having a good time at the cottage! So you need us to be secret friends. No problem! I can be very low-key. No one will notice us!"

"That's not—"

A triangle of light illuminated them briefly as the screen door to the cottage opened.

"Lucas, time to go!" Hanna held a container of leftovers in her arms, as well as the empty and cleaned jug of iced tea. Lucas bounced onto all fours, throwing the blanket toward Bee.

"Maybe we'll be able to see some meteors next time?" he asked. "See you later!"

Great. Bee listened to their fading footsteps, drawing the blanket over herself and turning to face the lake as the trampoline bounced from his movement.

Dots of light, not unlike the meteors that had never showed up, peppered the forest in clusters where other cottagers were enjoying the evening, either tucked into a good book in the coziness of indoors or sitting around campfires. The haunting sound of a loon's call echoed over the water as Bee's gaze landed on the inky blackness of the abandoned lot.

I wonder what I'll find there.

Was there a cottage still standing, or was it a pile of rubble? Would there be a usable firepit and the past remnants of a garden? The image of a gigantic gingerbread house crept up from the back of her mind, and she shuddered. *No, that was just a dream.* The only thing Bee knew for certain was that the lot hadn't been occupied in a very, *very* long time.

Her vision blurred as she continued to watch the lake, merging the water, the forest, and the sky. And then, in the center of the inky blackness, a light flickered on in the abandoned lot.

Bee's eyes flew wide open, searching. Her heart hammered in her chest. *What was that? What did I just see?*

But it had only been for an instant. And it was already gone.

· 5 ·

Bee's Mom Plans
a Surprise

Bee couldn't get that flicker of light out of her head, and the thought of it, the mystery, kept her from having a good night's sleep. Every few hours, she'd shake awake to peer through her window and into the night, in hopes of seeing something else. But there wasn't anything else to see, except sometime around five o'clock, when dawn turned the black sky gray and mist rose up to obstruct her view. *I need to get down there!*

Bee was out the door before anyone else had woken up or could ask her to help out with chores (she'd learned her lesson from yesterday). She tiptoed past both her parents' and Granny's bedrooms. Carefully pulled an oversize flannel shirt from the door hook. And slowly opened the screen door, wincing as the hinges creaked.

It was quiet out, too early even for the birds to start their chorus, and the world felt as though it belonged to Bee and Bee alone. Picking her way over the slippery grass, she moved through the mist toward the dock, wiping away the droplets that clung to her eyelashes. The silver of the canoe was barely visible nestled among the long stalks of cattails with their fuzzy brown tops. Cattails were a marvelous aquatic species, filtering silt from the water and offering a sheltered habitat for frogs and birds and fish (apparently, once properly prepared, the roots could even be eaten!). But as Bee dragged the canoe out from the forest of green stems into deeper water, a wailing cry pierced the air.

She stumbled back onto the wet dock, letting go of the canoe as the mist rose ever so slightly. It was almost like someone, or something, had howled into her ear. Her breath came out in short bursts as the canoe's full form became visible and a dark shape materialized on the boat's bow.

Sleek black feathers, a chest of white pearls, and dark red eyes. Bee inhaled sharply, and then sighed with relief.

"It's just a loon," she said to herself, and rose steadily to her feet, making shooing motions with her arms. "Get out of here, little guy!"

It didn't budge, simply cocking its delicate head to one side as if to get a better look at Bee. That was just a silly thought, of course, but Bee had to admit it was odd to see a loon settled completely out of the water on a boat, refusing to move as though it were standing guard. But it was going to take more than a loon to stop Bee. The canoe creaked as she stepped into it, locating the life jacket under the woven seat. And all the while, the beady red eyes didn't leave her.

Can loons go silly? Do rabid loons exist? Images of ducks foaming at the mouth came to mind, and then the disemboweled rodent she found by the lake's edge, making her shudder. And then she shivered again as the apparently soaking-wet life jacket seeped marshy water into her shirt. *Gross!* Bee shrugged it off, and only then did she notice a thin layer of water gurgling up through a cluster of tiny holes along the bottom of the canoe. *Oh no!* Tiny holes that would have quickly let in lake water and filled up the boat if she had attempted to paddle out. How had this happened? She'd been super careful yesterday!

The loon seemed to ruffle its feathers in quiet contentment, and for a second Bee considered its sharp beak and strong neck, then looked back at the holes, then back at the loon . . . and wondered.

Nah! Bee grimaced. *Don't be ridiculous.*

The mist was slowly dissipating, and little by little the sky turned from gray to orange to blue. Bee peered at the neighbors' dock and the glint of their red (and hopefully hole-free) canoe. Maybe she could just borrow that one instead? But the sounds of other cottagers stepping onto their docks with their morning coffees floated from across the lake, and the creak of the screen door sounded behind her.

"Binita! Can you come here?" her mom called from the cottage. "I need your help with an errand."

Reluctantly, Bee pushed the canoe back into the cattails. Exploring was going to have to wait until she could find another boat.

The car's tires crunched over the gravel as Bee's mom expertly navigated around tight corners and down steep hills until they were back on smooth asphalt road.

"The farmers' market?" Bee asked. "Why do you want to go to the farmers' market? And why are you wearing your salwar kameez?"

Sequins glittered along the length of the long dark dress and matching scarf. And for a pop of color, Mrs. Bakshi had paired the ensemble with emerald silk pants.

"Do you like it?" her mom asked, slowing as they entered the sleepy township of Storm. "I thought it would make Granny happy. And we're getting her favorite fruits today—nectarines and peaches are in season."

Bee couldn't argue with that. August was prime time for peaches, and nothing quite beat biting into the silky flesh of a perfectly ripened peach on a sunny afternoon. She could already feel the juices running down her chin, and the thought was enough to quell any further questions.

Her neglected phone buzzed as missed texts suddenly came through, and Bee scrolled through her messages excitedly. What was the Betsy Chillers amusement park like? Was it as creepy as the books?

The text blinked to life against the white backdrop.

> Beeee! I can't believe your embarrassing
> weird-o-rama family is forcing you to go to
> that stinky cottage instead of letting you
> come with us. They're so cheap.

Bee chewed the inside of her lip. *They're so cheap.* Kitty wasn't wrong, but it didn't feel great to read that. Then again, being friends with Kitty was the only thing saving Bee from total social implosion. She was grateful that Kitty wanted to be friends with her at all—in spite of Bee's parents and everything else. The nugget of hurt disappeared and Bee's lips stretched into a grin. She was lucky to have Kitty.

Totally, she wrote back. How's the park btw? Totally weird-o-rama without me?

Instantly she regretted the question. What if Kitty didn't miss her? What if she was having the best time of her life and finally decided to drop Bee from her circle? Bee waited anxiously as the three dots on her phone pulsed, indicating Kitty was typing. But then they disappeared.

The only thing worse than a rejection: no response at all.

Mrs. Bakshi parked on the side of what looked like a main road and led them on foot to a large parking lot at the back of the shopping strip. It didn't look like there would be anything back there, but Bee knew better than to question her mother's razor-sharp instincts for fresh produce and, of course, good deals.

Green canopies flapped lazily in the wind over long plastic tables piled with all the fresh fruits and veggies a heart could desire. There was even a stall full of long-stemmed sunflowers, a favorite of the beautiful red cardinal and vibrant blue jay. And there was already a good number of people strolling about, wicker baskets and reusable cotton bags in hand.

"Hey, Mom," Bee said as she followed her through the stalls, sidestepping a lady with a dog and passing a couple deep in conversation at a table offering garden tool sharpening services. The shiny metal edges of hedge clippers and branch loppers winked dangerously. "Mom, could you maybe not do that thing this time?"

"What thing?" Mrs. Bakshi stopped in front of a peach stall, surveying the baskets with a knowledgeable eye. "Oh, these are going to be perfect for a big batch of pickles!"

Bee bit her lip. When her family talked about pickle,

it wasn't the usual sweet-and-sour dunked-in-brine kind. Pickles, from what she knew about Indian cuisine, were a whole food group in itself. And somehow the best kind were made with slightly unripe fruit dunked in oils, chili, and lots of salt. Delicious but very—how should she put it—distinctly aromatic. Which was why Bee had banned pickles from her school lunch boxes long ago.

"You know your grandma came up with the peach pickle recipe when she found out how expensive mangoes were here?" her mom continued. "I was thinking freshly pickled peaches will make such good gifts, too!"

She began chatting with the vendor about the week's forecasted weather (apparently a large storm was going to hit the area that night, putting even the most seasoned cottagers on edge) and ignored Bee's hand tugging her scarf. *Please don't say it, please don't say it.* And then, the inevitable question came.

"Is it really that much for peaches? Even the unripe ones?" her mom asked. "What's your best price?"

Bee squeezed her eyes shut at her mom's tagline. *What's your best price?* Mrs. Bakshi loved a good bargain, sometimes a little too much. It wasn't enough that they salvaged bikes from the trash or got most of their clothes secondhand. No, Bee's mom just had to go and announce it every chance she got. Announce that they were cheap. *So embarrassing.* Bee raised the collar of her checkered flannel shirt despite the heat.

And then something caught her eye. A flash of red,

behind the corn stall. *What in the—* Bee peered across the market, scanning the growing crowd and mounds of fresh produce.

There it was again! A flash of red. *Wait a second.* Bee took a few steps forward, watching as a familiar boy with vibrant red hair poked his head from behind a vending table, looked left and right through his goggles with what stealth he could muster, then somersaulted down toward the next table. Lucas must have been playing some game, but his expression said he was taking it very, very seriously. Bee stifled a giggle.

Now that's *embarrassing.*

"Binita, did you hear that? What a coincidence!" her mom crowed.

The basket of peaches thumped against Bee's chest as her mother handed them to her for carrying. Bee turned to face her and the peach vendor, a noodly young man with a baseball cap pulled low over his shaggy blond hair and pimply face. The hat read "Happy Valley Peaches Farm."

"What's a coincidence?" Bee asked.

"Eli and his family used to live next door to the Gladers!" she exclaimed, as though the news was the discovery of the century.

Eli grimaced, revealing a mouth full of shiny braces, and brought a hand behind his head awkwardly. "My folks just moved out of the ol' cottage, sure. But I haven't been there in years. Stopped going a while back."

Bee's mom laughed the way she did when conversations didn't go the way she anticipated. "Oh, I can't imagine why you'd possibly want to be away from such a beautiful lake. It's simply idyllic. We're only here for the week, mind you, so we're just getting a taste of the cottage life. I guess after a few years, things might seem different. . . ."

"They sure do, ma'am," Eli replied tightly.

She continued on for a bit with well-wishes and more innocuous comments about the approaching storm, as Bee kept her gaze on the ground. There was a peach there, skin split and flesh bruised. It must have fallen off the table at some point, and no one noticed. Bee watched with curiosity as something wriggled out from inside, pushing peach juices to the surface. Two bug eyes popped out as a beetle ate its way to the surface.

Bee's mom patted her arm and she flinched. When she looked up, her mom was beginning to make her way to the next produce stall.

"See you around, then, and stay safe tonight," Eli said as Bee tore her eyes away from the beetle just in time to see a shadow settle over his expression.

Fear etched itself along the teen's brow. And then his dark eyes found hers for a split second and his lips moved so quickly Bee almost didn't catch the words. Words that would have given the creeps to even the legendary Betsy Chillers. Her fingers tingled and her chest tightened.

She could have sworn he said, "Keep off the water."

· 6 ·

Bee Doesn't Do as She's Told

They spent a few more minutes in the market, Mrs. Bakshi trying to get the best bargain and Bee trying to get rid of the chill that ran down her back. *What could Eli be scared of? What did he mean by "keep off the water"? And why did he look directly at me?* And most of all, she wondered if it could have anything to do with the abandoned lot she'd discovered.

Bee's mom opened the car trunk to place their market bounty inside. Fresh corn from the surrounding farms, tomatoes and leafy greens, carrots that still had a coat of dirt on them (freshly pulled that morning!), a tray of baked molasses cookies from a nice-looking lady who ran a bakery in town, and of course a full crate of unripe peaches for pickle-making.

Bee raced around to the passenger-side door, waiting for her mom to unlock it. She needed to get to that abandoned lot, now more than ever.

"We're not going back yet, Binita, sorry," her mom said, looking both ways before leading them across the road. "I have another errand to run."

They strode along the cracked sidewalk toward a squat store with drawings of colorful balloons spray-painted along the front window. Bee looked up to read the sign, frowning.

PARTY MANIA–YOUR ONE-STOP SHOP FOR ALL PARTY SUPPLIES

"Mom, this is a party shop. I don't think this is the right store."

"No, this is exactly right," she said, pulling the door open with a jingle of her bangles and holding it for Bee. "It's also why I wanted to make a big batch of that special peach pickle. It would be so nice to share with all the other cottagers when they come over."

Bee grimaced. She couldn't think of anything less fun. "And *why* would anyone be coming over?"

Mrs. Bakshi had on a mischievous smile, which made Bee's senses tingle with alarm.

"At the end of the week, we're going to throw a big party for Granny!"

WHAT? Bee nearly yelped out loud right then and

there in the entryway of the party shop. *A party for Granny?*

Her neck grew hot at the thought of a bunch of strangers sitting around a table, wondering how many more nature factoids her dad was going to share, while her mom naively passed out samosas and bhaji. Or worse, when she doled out *peach pickle party favors.* Bee shuddered. What would they think?

Somehow, she was able to keep her outburst tucked inside until they reached the car and were back on the road. A safe distance from the crowd, Bee felt the worries churning inside her, even louder than the car rattling over gravel.

"Do we have to, Mom?" Bee whined. "These are Granny's friends. Not ours. Why can't we wait until we're back home and you can invite your regular friends?"

Bee remembered celebrating Granny's birthday each year from the safety of their backyard garden.

"I want it to be special this year," her mom said, keeping her eyes peeled for the elusive cottage road exit. "Anyways, I *was* going to have another celebration once we're back home as well."

"*Two* parties? *Mo-om.*" Bee rolled her eyes, trying to quell the nervous gurgles in her belly. Or was that hunger?

Bee eyed the platter of molasses cookies resting in the back seat, savoring the warm sweetness in the car.

The cookies slid to the right under their wrapping as they made the turn onto the gravel path. If only her parents were the type to serve something like this at a party, or maybe lilac macarons and peppermint chocolates. Those were Kitty's favorites, and a staple at any of her birthdays. Bee checked her phone, her heart thudding when she saw she had an unread message. She opened it.

Instantly her stomach sank. Another picture, this time of Kitty with her arms around two other girls dressed head to toe in Betsy Chillers merch and brandishing slime-colored cotton candy. The caption, which Kitty underlined with sparkly heart stickers, felt like a thorn sinking into Bee's foot: *New day, new friends.*

"They look good, don't they," Mrs. Bakshi said, pulling Bee's eyes from her screen. At first she thought her mother had seen the picture, but Mrs. Bakshi's eyes were on the cookies in the rearview. "I thought it would be nice if you went to the neighboring cottagers to invite them to the celebration and offer them a few cookies at the same time. Isn't that a sweet idea?"

She winked at Bee, who was now so uncomfortably warm in her flannel shirt that she cranked on the car's AC without asking permission. *Why don't you hand them out yourself, since it's your party? Why do you have to involve me?* Plus, it felt like false advertising. There certainly wasn't going to be anything resembling molasses cookies at the party. But of course Bee didn't say any of that. The same way she sent a slew of starry-eyed emojis and carnival food stickers to Kitty instead of what she really felt. Which was much more like the barfing emoji.

As her mother brought in the groceries, Bee stood frowning and grumbling on the gravel path with her platter of plastic-wrapped cookies, instructed to stay away from the cottage until all deliveries and invitations had been made.

Bee listened to the creak of the screen door as her parents brought in the last of the food, and the forest went back to mostly being quiet.

Delivering the cookies was the last thing in the world she wanted to do right now. Knocking on strangers' doors, facing their confused looks, trying to explain that she wasn't selling anything but was inviting them to a cottage party. But not the Bakshis' cottage; their friends' cottage. What kind of party? Oh, you know, the kind where you get jars of peach pickle at the end. *So. Embarrassing.* Bee inhaled deeply.

The molasses cookies smelled delicious and the lake sparkled cerulean between the trees. Sure, Eli had warned her to stay off the water, but Eli didn't have to contend with her parents. And Bee had an idea.

What if I deliver the cookies, starting with the abandoned lot? I mean, I don't know if it's abandoned for real. And then . . . I could accidentally leave the cookies there.

It was an awfully mean idea. Bee's heart leaped into her throat as the inevitable scenarios played out in her head. Her parents would be planning for this big party all week. The kitchen would be a bonanza of traditional dishes. The decorations and outdoor furniture would be all set out. And the day of, when no one showed up, her mom would take one look at Bee and know she was hiding something. And Bee wouldn't be able to meet her gaze, because of course there would be no explanation good enough, and then—

No. Bee stopped her train of thought. She stared across the lake, feeling something stir inside her. She frowned. The party was her mom's idea, her mom's thing. Why should she have to give out the invitations? Plus, there was going to be a second party for Granny back home, right? So it wasn't that big of a deal if this one turned out to be a bust, right?

Bee gripped the plate of cookies tightly, hardly able to believe what she was about to do. But she'd made up her mind. Checking over her shoulder for witnesses and finding only a chattering chipmunk, she crouched behind the family car, snuck around the guesthouse and the outhouse (which smelled like the scene of a real horror story), and then raced to the wood shelter, where the Gladers collected wood from downed trees on their property, drying and storing the logs for their living room wood burner. Two red hummingbird feeders filled to the brim with sugar water hung on either side of the sloped roof.

Bee chewed her lip. The next bit involved walking in plain sight of the cottage's big front window, with nowhere to duck or creep. But her parents would be busy for at least the next few minutes putting away the groceries, and facing away from the window. . . . *This might just work out!*

Bee bolted, streaking across the lawn with the cookies held out in front of her, leaping over the few stairs that led to the sandy water, and stole through the strip of cattails that separated their dock from the Joneses'. And there, floating lazily in the still water, was the bright red canoe, which was hole-free and—bonus!—loon-free as well. Bee wasn't the kind of person who would normally take someone else's canoe out on the water without asking first, but she wasn't having a normal kind of day. *I'll apologize later,* she promised herself, *to both the neighbors and to Mom.* And in less than a few seconds, Bee secured the cookies in the bottom of the canoe, zipped up her life jacket, and pushed off into the lake.

Her heart drummed in her chest, but it wasn't a scared feeling. It was a feeling of excitement. Bee made sure to get in a few good paddle strokes before looking back. Thankfully, there was no sign of her parents, only Granny's slumped little form, asleep in an Adirondack chair.

The water parted easily, the gurgle of the little whirlpools kissing the sides of the canoe with each of

Bee's strokes as she made straight for the tangle of white branches. In the distance, she counted two—no, three—dark shapes surfacing. Three loons. She tensed as their red eyes found her. Were they going to attack? One of the loons spread its wings slowly and then beat the air, feathers flapping back and forth and water churning—like it was considering attacking . . . or trying to send a warning. But Bee couldn't be sure, and the loon settled back into the water with its buddies, scanning the deep for their next meal.

The canoe's bow touched the first of the branches and Bee stopped paddling, letting momentum carry her forward through the marsh and steering away from the bigger branches as needed. The putrid stink intensified as the canoe broke through the film of stagnant algae. And then the familiar bump of hitting land.

Placing her paddle horizontally across the canoe from edge to edge (a good trick to prevent unwanted dips into the lake), Bee carefully stood, leaning on the paddle and sliding it forward as she moved to keep her balance. Once at the front of the canoe, she stepped under the wall of cedars onto land. The wind forced the trees to wave, blowing away the stink and filling the air with the soft lap of waves against the shoreline.

The pine needles and cedar twigs on the ground came away easily with a sweep of her feet, exposing a cobblestone patio beneath, where a small wrought-iron table and matching chair rested. Once upon a time, this was surely where the past owners used to sit, sipping chai in the late morning and looking over the lake. *What a relaxing place.*

After securing the canoe to a nearby trunk and placing the offensive invitation cookies in the center of the little table (after stashing a few in her pockets, of course), Bee advanced, walking deeper into the abandoned property.

She passed old tires that lay scattered around what used to be a manicured lawn, with sprigs of dried weeds sprouting out in great tufts where herbs and flowers might have grown.

The lower bank was separated from the main cottage by a large stone retaining wall made of yellowed sandstone and crumbling mortar. On one side, moss sprouted from the cracks and a trickle of water streamed down the rocks and off to the side of the property toward the lake. On the other was a narrow flagstone staircase with a rounded overarching trellis.

How pretty! Bee could practically see how the rosebushes would have climbed over the wooden arch once upon a time, turning it into a flowery, aromatic doorway. She picked her way up the stairs, her feet scuffing the dried leaves, and gasped as the old house came into view.

Even in its charred, half-standing state, the building was impressive. Bee cautiously stepped through the doorless doorway into the roofless building, trailing a finger along the peeling striped wallpaper. Built on a steep slope, the thick stone walls traced out the remnants of a first floor that used to hold a grandiose entryway. As she moved through it, the leftover iron grating of the fireplace swung on its last hinge. Bee kicked up the ashes and watched them fall back down like gray snow onto her shoes, then marveled at a thin young maple snaking up from the crumbling firewood, its trunk curved in its quest for sunlight.

A little farther in rested the remains of a huge kitchen, with cracked marble countertops and a huge cast-iron oven surrounding a small sinkhole with a stream running through it. Bee climbed her way carefully toward it, reveling in the softness of the moss on her hands and the clear, cold, pooling water.

It's so . . . beautiful.

The sun was getting hot, chasing the shadows from the building's crevices and heating the old stone. Bee removed her flannel shirt and shoes, found a comfortable ledge on the smooth marble, and dipped her feet into the pool. The relief was instant, soothing and invigorating all at once.

She surveyed her little spot of paradise happily, making short work of the first molasses cookie and then savoring the second one slowly as she wiggled her toes in the water. This was the perfect getaway, the ideal secret hideout.

It didn't explain the flash of light she'd seen, but

there was certainly nothing too spooky to find here. She'd definitely have to add a haunted detail or two when she texted Kitty about it later.

Bee had just brought the last delicious morsel of cookie to her mouth when a lone cloud momentarily covered the sun, sending a cold shiver up the length of her spine.

"Where did you get that?" a voice whispered through the trees. "That better not be gingerbread."

· 7 ·

The Gingerbread Witch

Bee gasped, accidentally inhaling the mouthful of cookie, which sent her into a coughing and spluttering fit. The voice wasn't from the trees at all, but from a girl about Bee's age, with dark ringlets and large dark eyes set in light brown skin and one leg up on Bee's marble perch. She wore an old-fashioned dress shirt tucked into long khaki shorts, which made her look almost like a pirate. Her delicate face formed a pout, brow furrowed and hands on her hips.

There was something about her that reminded Bee of Kitty—that I-don't-care-what-other-people-think-of-me attitude that often led to sharp words and hurt feelings, if you weren't on the right side of the fence. But also of someone else. Someone she knew very well but couldn't quite put her finger on.

"Al?" Bee asked hesitantly once she stopped choking, remembering the name Lucas's mom had mentioned at dinner.

She'd only seen her once, at a distance, but there was no mistaking her. The girl squinted suspiciously, then took a long sniff of the air the way dogs do when catching a scent. But the sniff seemed to satisfy her, because the frown disappeared and her face relaxed into a smirk.

"Molasses, not gingerbread," she said, taking a seat beside Bee next to the small pool. "The name's Alina, by the way."

Alina.

Bee watched with surprise as Alina removed her shoes one at a time, then threw them over her head and into the rubble.

"Won't your mom get mad if you lose your shoes?" Bee asked.

Alina tilted her head back, the ringlets cascading down the small of her back, and let out a single bark of a laugh.

"Ha! My parents let me do whatever I want." She turned to face Bee, crossing her legs. "That's why I spend so much time here. My secret hideaway."

Bee watched as Alina's smile widened and her dark eyes sparkled like the lake on a sunny day. Alina was pretty cool, and thankfully wasn't into wearing ghost specs like her brother.

"I wish my parents were more relaxed about me doing things like exploring," Bee said.

Alina nodded vigorously. "Exploring is my favorite thing. I need to be *out there*, you know? Finding new trails, discovering hidden treasures. Life would be so boring being stuck with *family*, doing boring *family* things."

"Like going to dinner parties?" Bee joked.

Alina stuck out her tongue and then burst out into a fit of giggles. Bee heard herself joining in. Between the cold water on her legs and the hot sun on her face . . . For some reason—Bee couldn't explain it—she felt good around Alina, comfortable. Like catching up with an old friend she hadn't seen since summer camp years earlier. She definitely knew her, but from where?

It took a while before they could catch their breath again.

"My mom used to try to make me do things," Alina said. "But she learned to stop. She learned that it was best to let me do things my way. And I love it here."

"Yeah," Bee agreed. "I've been wanting to come up here and explore since last night . . ." She glanced at Alina, who was already back to splashing her feet in the pool, wetting the hems of Bee's capris. "Since I saw a light."

Alina stopped moving, and there wasn't a hint of a smile on her face. Bee's cheeks flushed and her scalp tingled.

"You've seen it, too, haven't you?" Bee breathed, feeling the weight of the mystery press in a bit closer. *I'm not the only one.*

"Course I have, I'm an explorer."

Alina jerked out of the pool, skipped over the rubble, scrambled up what was left of a stairwell beside the front entrance, and perched on the remains of a balcony. There she stood, hands on her hips again, facing the wind and the lake, and Bee thought all that was missing was a large floppy hat and a ship's steering wheel.

"I pay attention to everything. Especially the details," she yelled out.

Cautiously, Bee followed suit, barefoot. She left her overshirt and shoes on the marble by the pool and picked her way through the rubble, which, she discovered, was mostly bedded with dead leaves, pine needles, and moss.

"It feels like I'm walking on carpet," Bee said, feeling herself break out in a bold grin. "My parents would go ballistic if they knew what I was doing."

Her foot found the smooth oak of the first step, sending a wailing creak through the rest of the staircase that seemed to move like a shudder through the entire house carcass. Like ripples when you step on a floating dock.

"Let them." Alina smirked, reaching down for Bee's hand.

With a deep breath, Bee raced up the stairs as the

creaks loudened and joists groaned, and grabbed hold of Alina's arm. Everything grew quiet as soon as her feet touched the warm stone of the balcony.

"You can be you here—the version of yourself *you* want to be," Alina said. "There isn't a better thing in the world."

She squeezed Bee's hand and then let go, and Bee felt a tiny piece of herself click into place, a perfect fit.

From their high perch, Bee could see above the wall of cedars to the lake and the other cottages along its shoreline. The two kayakers from the day before were doing another loop, the orange and red streaking through the blue water. Some kids a few cottages down were shrieking wildly as they took turns cannonballing. She even thought she could see the milling forms of her parents, jogging back and forth across the lawn.

Oh no, they're looking for me. A pang of guilt hit her in the chest again at the thought of Granny's party. Followed by another pang. Did she make the right decision, crossing the lake and not giving out the cookie invitations? In any case, Bee needed to get back soon— the last thing she wanted to do was worry her parents. But somehow, it felt wrong admitting it in front of someone like Alina.

"Maybe you could come hang out at my place sometime? At the Gladers', I mean." Bee hesitated. She hoped very much that Alina would want to hang out again. "We can . . . build forts, and catch frogs, and that sort of thing, if you like. . . . And we have a trampoline! And there's lots of places to explore along the gravel paths."

Alina shrugged. "I don't know. This is my favorite place to explore, right here. Plus, I don't usually hang out with people who can't stand up to their weird-o-rama parents."

Bee's smile fell a little.

"And you should know," Alina continued, "I try to stay away from the neighbors' cottage." She leaned in, lowering her voice. "It's not *safe*."

Bee watched Alina's wide eyes. Was she scared? What could someone like Alina possibly be scared of?

"Why isn't it safe?" Bee asked, unsure if she wanted to hear the answer herself.

The lone cry of a loon called out, reverberating madly around the lake. Her father's words came back to her: *call-up-a-storm*.

"Why isn't it safe, Alina?" she asked again.

Alina's eyes got all serious. When her eyebrows pinched in the middle, Bee's heart quickened, and when she spoke, it sounded like the wind in the trees.

"The Gingerbread Witch."

Bee's breathing shallowed, the sweet spice suddenly filling her nostrils. This wasn't like Lucas's ghost games. Images from her dream flashed before her eyes—the gingerbread house erupting from Hanna's platter and transforming into a life-size cottage. The jelly bean shingles, the chocolate-bark door, the thudding of her heart.

"Like, a *real* witch?"

"Well, what would *you* call an old lady who catches kids and bakes them in her oven?" Alina asked.

A sun-bleached trailer and a shaggy brown overcoat and a reddish beetle skuttling over an eyeball crossed Bee's mind. She swallowed hard. A bead of sweat trickled down her hairline. So there was a witch living in the cottaging community of Storm Lake. She closed her fingers into fists to stop the tremble in her hands.

"I . . . I think I've seen her."

"Of course you have," Alina breathed. "She doesn't hide. That would make parents suspicious. But she's out there, mark my words, waiting for me. So it's better if you don't tell anyone where I am."

She'd come across a witch or two in Betsy Chillers books, which, of course, were completely fictional stories. But there was always something at the back of her mind, questioning: Where did the stories come from, if it was all pretend?

Playing around the cottage was definitely out of the question, then. "Well," Bee said, "then I guess I can meet you here again tomorrow? If I ask my parents . . . I mean, I'm sure they'll be all right with me exploring if they know I'm with you."

Alina smiled widely. "Parents are such a bore. You need to stand up to them, tell them what you're really thinking. They can't boss you around forever."

Bee pursed her lips, trying to imagine her mom's expression if she so much as pushed back on washing the dishes.

Alina tilted her head, letting a wisp of her ringlets brush Bee's shoulder. "If your parents are going to be a problem, it's going to be difficult for us to hang out."

"No, no, they won't be a problem," Bee stuttered, her pulse quickening. For some reason, the thought of losing this chance to become friends with Alina made her stomach knot.

"You're cooler than I thought," Alina quipped. "I didn't think you had it in you. I'm impressed." Then her smile dipped slightly at the edges. "But that's not the only problem. There are these loons, you see. I think the witch sent them after me. Is there any way you can figure out how to get rid of them?"

"I can try," Bee said without thinking. How hard could it be to swat away a few lake birds, anyway? "So does that mean we can hang out?"

"If you can deal with the loons . . . maybe." Her eyelashes fluttered like moth wings. "Meet me at the abandoned lot once the sun is set and your parents are asleep. Then we'll see about investigating this strange light."

Going out on the lake at night? Sneaking around? Her parents *definitely* wouldn't approve. And that gave Bee a strange kind of thrill that hummed from her heart right down to her toes. There was only one issue left.

"What about the witch?" Bee's breath caught in her throat. "Will she know I'm helping you?"

Alina sighed, her delicate shoulders sloping down farther with her breath. "Probably." Then her smile turned sharper than a fire-poking stick and her eyes grew harder than granite. "So make sure you don't get caught."

· 8 ·

Sneaking Out
After Dark

Even though she put on a brave face in front of Alina, Bee had never snuck out after dark in her entire life. In fact, her parents had only recently agreed to push her bedtime to eight o'clock! So when her mom peeked her nose into Bee's bedroom to turn the lights off for the night, Bee was a right mess of nerves.

Mrs. Bakshi raised an eyebrow, already changed into her colorful satin pajamas inherited from some great-aunt. "Are you all right, Binita?"

Bee grimaced, sinking as far under the blankets as she could to hide her reddening cheeks.

"I'm fine. Good night," she said in her best I'm-definitely-not-about-to-sneak-out voice. *Do they suspect anything? Does Mom already know?* She'd held strong and kept it a secret that she hadn't given out the cookie invitations. She could do this, too.

"Are you sure?" her mom asked. "If there's something bothering you, you can tell me."

She lingered in the doorway with a finger hovering near the light switch, using that annoying tone parents use when they're trying to pull information out of you. Bee felt her chest tighten and the confession slowly inch out, but shook her head. No, not this time. Not when her parents were the only thing stopping her from hanging out with Alina.

Bee plastered on a smile and stared pointedly at the ceiling light. "No, I'm fine. Can you get the lights?"

"All right, then."

Bee blinked as they went out, the fuzzy image of the lightbulb slowly fading from her vision as darkness rushed into the corners of the room. It was a cloudy night—the kind that promised storms. Although according to her dad, who always disagreed with the weather forecast, this wasn't the *big* storm.

"*If* it rains," he'd said, lowering his voice ominously to get a rise out of Bee, "it would only be a taste of what's to come."

She rolled her eyes at the memory. Either way, there was no helping light coming from the stars or the moon, so it took a while for Bee's eyes to adjust.

Finally, once she could no longer hear the rustle of her parents moving through the cottage, it was time.

Bee took a shaky breath and stepped out of bed. The floor was cool under her feet as she tiptoed around the room, getting dressed as quietly as possible (which was pretty difficult in the dark). Her toe caught on the bottom of a dresser and Bee let out a yelp before clamping her hands over her mouth.

Her heartbeat quickened as she listened for the telltale sounds of her parents getting out of bed as the pain in her toe dissipated. Thankfully, the cottage was deathly quiet. Bee breathed out slowly. *Note to self—next time you sneak out, go to bed fully dressed!* Then she smiled as she crept into the living room, surprised at herself. Somehow, she already knew there would be a next time.

After opening multiple drawers in the kitchen and checking under various pillows, Bee finally located a working flashlight. It was time. She placed both hands on the screen door and pushed.

A strident *creak!* resonated through the air as the rusty hinges grated against each other, followed quickly by voices from the bedroom. Bee's heart leaped into her throat as the inevitable scenarios played out in her head. Her mom would ask her what in the world she was doing, and of course there would be no explanation good enough, and then—

No. Bee stopped her train of thought, the same way she had stopped it earlier when she was supposed to be handing out cookies and inviting the neighbors over. *I want to see Alina.* There was a strange feeling in the pit of her stomach, almost like . . . hunger. *And I'm going to see her no matter what.*

Bee bolted through the door and let it swing shut behind her with another loud creak. She ran across the dark grass and past the trampoline without looking back. She cut through the small thicket of cattails to the neighbors' dock and climbed into the canoe.

Finally, Bee stopped to take a breath. Her chest was moving up and down as though she'd run to town and back instead of simply a few feet. A drop of sweat clung to her frizzy hair. But she was here, and she'd made it. She'd snuck out.

Bee gazed across the lake, which was as dark as the sky. No, not completely dark. There were wavering lines of silver here and there, like the shiny black screen of her cell phone when she went too long without charging it. The lake was reflecting the light from something. . . . Bee brought her gaze farther across the lake, where strange lights flickered from the abandoned lot.

A giddy anticipation started to build. What were those lights? What would she and Alina find? What—

"What the!" Bee let out a gasp as lake water washed over her sandals. Lake water, in the bottom of the neighbors' canoe. Lake water, flooding in through tiny holes along the bottom. Exactly like the Gladers' canoe. *Oh no, not again!* How was Bee supposed to cross the lake now? That was two canoes now mysteriously riddled with holes. Almost like someone didn't want her to cross.

A loon's cry sounded nearby, but in the darkness Bee couldn't see where it was. Goose bumps ran up her arms.

"Get away from me! Get away, you loons!"

She stepped back out of the canoe and waved her arms frantically. Mosquitoes whined in her ears. Another loon cry sounded, this time from behind her. And then a resounding crack. Like a branch breaking as something moved through the forest. Something that definitely wasn't a loon. Bee moistened her lips, finding her mouth suddenly very dry. Slowly, she lowered her arms and backed away, carefully placing one foot behind the other through the cattails that separated the properties. Exploring with Alina would have to wait until another time.

And then, Bee turned and ran as fast as she could back up the grass slope to the cottage.

· 9 ·

Albus the Ginger Cat

The next morning, Bee woke with a pit in her stomach.

It didn't matter that it was a day like any other, with blue skies and cotton candy clouds and just the right amount of breeze. She was extra cautious when she trudged out the creaking screen door arm in arm with Granny. She looked over her shoulder at regular intervals, double-checking every suspicious rustle from the forest floor and jumping at every whistle in the trees. And all the while, the pit in her stomach remained.

Granny clicked her tongue against the roof of her mouth, like Bee's mom did when there was something that bothered her. With newly painted nails, oversize glasses, and permed white hair, she truly looked like she was from a different century.

"Would you look at that," she exclaimed. "Your dad was right again. It didn't rain!"

When Bee didn't respond, Granny squeezed her arm between her hands. "You're full of beans today! Did the mosquitoes get you? Are you uncomfortable?"

Bee adjusted the black fleece pullover she'd dragged from the bottom of her backpack and then hopped on either foot to shake out the gravel from her sandals. She was uncomfortable, partly because she'd forgotten her overshirt and shoes by the small pool yesterday. She was on edge because her parents hadn't mentioned anything about hearing the screen door over breakfast, even though she was sure they knew she had snuck out. And she was disappointed that she hadn't been able to see Alina as planned.

But mostly she was scared of who might have been watching her last night—of who might be watching her still.

A wave of goose bumps swept over Bee's body. *The Gingerbread Witch*. A real witch who baked children and probably did other horrid things as well, who lived in a beat-up trailer a few kilometers up the road and traveled with a flock of sharp-beaked, red-eyed loons. Normally Bee would revel in the creepiness of it all, but after such a close encounter last night . . . Not even the thought of an adventure with Alina, with her resolute chin and confident dark eyes, could shake the dread from Bee's thoughts.

She tried to think of what Betsy Chillers would do in this kind of situation—maybe learn to speak to animals and then harness the powers of the local wildlife to launch a full-scale attack, or build a witch trap using Lucas as bait (no harm would come to him, of course). If this were a book, there would be no end to her options. But this wasn't a story safely confined to the bindings of a paperback. This was real.

She huddled closer to Granny as they shuffled down the gravel path, so entrenched in her own thoughts and paranoia that she barely heard when Granny started to talk.

"Are your mom and dad up to something? They've been oddly secretive lately, up to no good, in my opinion. You wouldn't happen to know anything about that, would you, Bee?"

Granny had always had a strangely acute sense of observation.

"Have they?" Bee shrugged innocently, even though she knew for a fact that her mom was crafting decorations for Granny's party at that very moment. "I hadn't noticed."

A monarch fluttered around milkweed plants by the path where some light managed to leak through the foliage. The white of a deer's tail flashed as it skirted away from the crunch of their footsteps.

By the time they shuffled back into the cottage, Granny was ready for a midmorning nap. Bee helped her into the house before taking a seat on the front porch, sinking deep into an Adirondack chair. What was it about them that was so comfortable? It felt like a big hug, and the angle of the seat made it all too easy to rest your head back and stare at the sky. But Bee was too on edge to relax today.

Alina's warning kept circling her head. *It's not safe.*

A hummingbird zipped through the property toward the feeders like a race car, and Bee gripped the chair's arms. A mosquito came to investigate near her ear, and she nearly slapped herself in the face. The bushes behind the wood shelter quivered. And then she heard it—the unmistakable crack of a branch snapping under someone's foot.

It's not safe.

Bee's pulse picked up speed, as though trying to keep pace with the hummingbird's wingbeats. She looked back to the safety of the cottage. It would only take her a second to jump from the chair to the screen door and huddle indoors where her dad was starting up lunch preparations. But Bee was frozen. Her legs heavy as lead, her vision blurry.

It's not safe.

The bushes quivered again, and Bee's knuckles turned white from strain. And then a tuft of flaming-red hair poked out of the foliage. *What?* Bee released her death-grip, pushing herself with difficulty out of the chair and rushing down the steps onto the grass.

"Lucas!" Bee yelped, her cheeks burning.

Lucas's ghostly face appeared from behind the wood shelter, a streak of dirt smudged across the bridge of his nose below his goggles. He nodded solemnly at Bee, looked left and right, and dashed across the yard toward her, crouched low to the ground. Funnily enough, the oddest thing about him today wasn't his excessively furtive behavior, but the large ball of disgruntled fluff that balanced precariously on his shoulder.

With stubby whiskers and a smooshed face and long fur that looked like it hadn't been brushed in weeks, the ginger tabby could have camouflaged perfectly in Lucas's hair. Except for the two bright green eyes that peered down at Bee, who was having a hard time focusing on anything else. Strangely human eyes.

Of course he walks around with a cat on his back, she thought. There was never an individual who stood out *more* than Lucas, and Bee felt her lip curl in annoyance.

"What in the world are you doing?" Bee finally managed to ask.

Lucas grinned. "Shortcut!"

"And why wouldn't you come down the driveway like a normal person?"

"I thought you wanted to be secret friends," Lucas

answered, as the cat pushed affectionately into the side of his head.

"I just . . . ," Bee started to respond, then stopped.

Lucas was secret friends with her, and she was supposed to keep her friendship with Alina on the down-low. The thought of Alina made the pit in Bee's stomach stir. This was getting complicated. And a tiny part of Bee felt like it wasn't right.

"Well . . . ," Bee said, feeling a little bit at odds. Lucas ruffled the cat's ears and scratched under its chin, and the cat purred nearly as loud as a motorboat. "Well, what's with the . . . cat?"

She had to physically stop herself from adding the word *creepy*. Because come on, the cat was totally creepy!

Lucas promptly grabbed hold of the big fuzzy thing and held it out—claws, fangs, and all—toward Bee to hold. "She's loads friendly."

Bee stepped back politely, watching the cat cautiously and trying hard not to throw herself up the stairs (she could never be sure if a cat was about to lash out, but she knew for a fact that they were thinking about it).

"Oh, that's all right." She grimaced as the strange green eyes followed hers a little too closely. *Creepy, creepy, creepy.* "You can keep her on your shoulder. She seems happier there."

Lucas shrugged and replaced the cat on her perch. "This is Albus. Al for short. My aunt got her for me from a rescue because no one wanted her. Can you believe it?"

Bee tried hard not to react, because as far as cats went, Albus was not a looker. *Al.* Bee frowned. *Same as his sister.* And there was something else, too. She stared hard at the pink nose and stubby whiskers.

"Albus is a she?" Bee asked.

The light shifted subtly, and it was almost like there was another pair of eyes staring back at her. It was those uncanny human eyes again.

"Yeah, funny story." Lucas grinned. "We thought Albus was a he when we first got her, then she had kittens. . . . Anyways, we gave the kittens away but the name stuck. And she's been my friend ever since." Lucas looked down to his cutoff sweatpants and sandals, the grin fading. "Sometimes she's my only friend."

Bee looked away, too, sweeping her hand over her hair and making sure there weren't too many flyaways. Trouble at school, Hanna had mentioned at the dinner party. Lucas had looked away then, too, which reminded Bee of all the times she'd had that exact same look. Thankfully, being chosen as Kitty's friend made all those things go away—the raised eyebrows, the sly glances, the muffled whispers behind cupped hands. But still, the thought of having something in common with Lucas was the opposite of good. *This is not the kind of friend I need right now. Or ever.* Bee sighed. If only she'd bumped into Alina instead.

"Anyways." His expression brightened, and Albus

gave a big wide yawn. "I thought we could do some-thing today. Anything you want to do? Right after I do my chores, that is. But hey, maybe you could help? It'll be fun!"

Bee pursed her lips, trying her best to look past the goggle eyes and the cat scarf. *It's not safe.* But being around Lucas made her feel a wee bit safer, and a wee bit more protected from sudden attacks of a witchy nature. Even the concept of witches felt a little bit less possible around Lucas's silliness, as though bad things couldn't possibly get near something so . . . annoying. It took Bee a moment to realize Lucas was still talking.

"We could explore the trails, or we could go swim-ming instead, it can get pretty hot—"

"No swimming," Bee cut in abruptly, then added, "because I don't have goggles. I forgot them back home."

She could only come up with so many excuses for why she didn't want to jump into the lake.

"Oh, that's too bad." Lucas pouted. "I wonder if we have an extra pair somewhere. I'm sure I could find one. Maybe after we patch up the canoe—"

Bee's ears tingled at the reminder of last night, and the loons, and what could have happened. Her ears also tingled with guilt, because of course she'd never gotten around to asking whether she could borrow Lucas and Hanna's canoe. She' d taken it without asking.

"What's wrong with your canoe?" Bee asked anx-iously, even though she had a pretty good idea.

But Lucas didn't seem to notice and simply shrugged. "It happens all the time around here. It's a real head-scratcher. Canoes, boats, you name it. If it floats, you can bet that sooner or later, these tiny holes are going to appear in the bottom. And they'll let the water in so slowly, you only notice once you're halfway out on the lake. Better to swim if you want to get anywhere around here."

Bee sucked up his words like an ice-cold mango lassi (that is to say, so fast she practically felt a brain freeze coming on). First the Gladers' canoe and then Lucas and Hanna's canoe last night? It wasn't a coincidence. Alina was right about the loons—they were definitely working for the witch. Bee let out a shaky breath as her goose bumps from the night before returned, despite the warmth. It could only mean one thing: the witch didn't want anyone crossing the lake. . . .

"Actually," Bee said, "I wouldn't mind helping patch up your canoe. Ours—I mean, the Gladers' canoe—is also leaking. Also . . . there's something else." As she talked, Lucas's eyes brightened and his hair seemed to glow even redder. "I seem to have a loon problem. You wouldn't know anything about loons, by chance, would you?"

It was a long shot, but anything was worth a try if it meant getting one step closer to seeing Alina again. Albus yawned and Bee crossed her arms as she waited.

"Loons, huh?" Lucas finally said. "There might be

something in the neighborhood shed that can help us. That place is packed with the weirdest things, from all the different renters and owners who ever lived around here. But I have to warn you"—Lucas scrunched his nose, and the smudged nose-dirt crumbled into powder and blew away—"it can get a bit weird in there."

"Weird?" Bee nearly huffed out a laugh at the thought of someone like Lucas finding anything weirder than himself. "Trust me, I can handle it. Let's go n—"

Their plans were interrupted by the creak of the screen door and the tantalizing aromas of curried potato masala and something fried. Her dad's cooking.

"Binita! Lunch is ready," Mrs. Bakshi called, poking her head out the screen door.

Bee briefly considered remaining where she was, hidden in the shadows of the deck. Lunch would be there when they got back. But Lucas had other plans, immediately jumping out into the open and plastering on a gigantic smile.

"Hello, Bee's mom, something smells good in there!"

Mrs. Bakshi did a very good job of not ogling the oddity that was Albus and smiled widely in return. After all, everyone knows there's nothing parents love more than a healthy appetite.

"Lucas, sweetie!" she exclaimed. "Please join us for lunch."

So much for secret friends. Bee sighed as Lucas turned to her with a please-can-we smile.

Her gaze slowly turned to the lake. To the dark pine and brambles and young oak and spindly maples and the blanket of dead leaves that covered the forest floor. It all seemed to be holding its breath, waiting.

The Gingerbread Witch.

When Alina had said it, her eyes had been so serious, as dark as the long ringlets that grazed Bee's shoulder. If things were that serious, that dangerous, shouldn't Alina have told her mother about it? But Bee already knew the answer to that question. Alina wasn't that kind of girl. She was the kind of girl who didn't ask her parents for permission, and skipped barefoot over sharp rubble (seriously, you shouldn't do this) and explored abandoned cottages after dark.

I can't tell my parents. Plus, there's no way they'd believe me.

What was more likely to happen was a mini interrogation as to why she was hanging out with Lucas's sister in a dilapidated house. Which would inevitably unearth the whole cookie-invitations-that-were-never-delivered debacle. A pang of guilt reverberated through Bee's chest before she remembered what Alina had said about not letting her parents boss her around.

"We're kind of busy, Mom," Bee said, her gaze still riveted on the lake. "We'll eat later."

"Later?" Mrs. Bakshi gasped as though delaying a meal was possibly the worst idea she'd ever heard. "But you might get hungry, dear! Just a second." She disappeared back into the cottage and returned with two dosas rolled up in tinfoil. "Here, you can eat on the go," she said with a smile.

Lucas didn't hesitate, grabbing his dosa burrito with both hands. "Thanks! This looks great!"

"Yeah, thanks," Bee echoed.

A breeze blew off the water, rustling the pine branches and tugging at the hem of Bee's shirt, like a reminder from across the lake. *Meet me at the abandoned lot, once the sun is set and your parents are asleep.* Because of the loons, Bee hadn't been able to sneak out last night to meet Alina, and she couldn't afford any more delays.

Distractedly, Bee turned away from the lake to accept her dosa. And as she did, she caught the cat's gaze as its head swiveled back toward the lake and its whiskers quivered.

As though the cat could hear Alina's words, too. And knew something was coming.

· 10 ·

Dosa and Danger

Dosa—a savory pancake-like dough fried to crispy goodness in ghee and wrapped around a filling of spiced potato and peas. From her earliest memories, layered over every birthday or holiday or visit from relatives were the delicious scents of her father's specialty dish—well, his *only* dish. But as Mr. Bakshi was fond of saying, "If you've only got one thing, you've got to get it right." It was Bee's favorite, and the type of meal that punctuated all Bakshi-family special occasions throughout the year. Or it used to be her favorite.

She'd invited her friends over for her birthday last year, and when the dosa came out, Kitty had politely pushed her plate away, batted her eyelashes, and asked

Bee's dad, "Are you sure there isn't *anything else* to eat?"

It was another warm day, already much warmer than it had been that morning. Reluctantly, Bee shrugged off her pullover, revealing yet another lightly bejeweled oversize T-shirt.

"Where to?" Bee asked as they paused at the cottage property line.

Albus meowed and Lucas licked leftover dosa ghee from the tips of his fingers before pointing left. (Bee had given Lucas her dosa as well. For some reason, even though she was hungry, she couldn't bring herself to eat her parents' cooking.)

Bee hesitated. She'd never turned left before, toward where all the other cottagers lived—her chest tightened the way it did sometimes when she got scared. But it wasn't a Betsy Chillers kind of scared. This fear came from inside. But she couldn't tell Lucas any of that, and he was already several strides gone. A warm wind came buffeting down the path, and a cold shiver ran up Bee's spine.

What's worse, bumping into other cottagers or bumping into the witch? She shoved her qualms to the side and followed Lucas.

"I can't believe you get along so well with my parents," Bee said, distracting herself. "Don't you think they're a bit . . . weird?"

It really was warm, the kind of warm where you

start dreaming of the condensation rolling off an ice-cold drink. Lucas stuck to the shadiest parts of the gravel trail.

"I don't know, I think they're kinda cool," he said matter-of-factly.

Bee chuckled, mostly from nerves, because they were passing someone's cottage, but also because she wasn't sure Lucas knew what "cool" meant. Certainly it wasn't the kind of thing he cared about, not like Alina. It was hard to believe they were even related, with her permanently wolfish grin and porcelain features. The mere thought of her tugged at Bee like a fishhook, and she was filled with so much anticipation for their next meeting that she almost didn't notice the couple walking hand in hand toward them.

Yikes! Bee's shoulders scooted so far up she might as well have been one of those painted turtles ducking into their shells at the first sight of danger. They were exactly the kind of people she imagined would live in a cottaging neighborhood like this one—dressed in loose-fitting khakis that most definitely were *not* secondhand, with sleek hair that somehow managed to remain unkinked despite the humidity.

Bee averted her gaze as they passed by, her ears burning hotter than a cast-iron pan on full heat, hoping the sound of lips stretching into smiles was all in her imagination. She repeated the mantra her mother had given her to avoid meltdowns on Saturday-morning shopping runs. *They aren't laughing at you; they probably didn't even notice you. They're probably too busy being nervous about what other people are thinking of them.*

"You know, when I get the squigglies, I pretend I'm in my favorite place." Lucas's hand grazed hers and Albus's large human eyes popped out from the curly, fuzzy mess of red.

"Squigglies?" Bee asked, her breath returning to normal as the couple's crunching footsteps faded away.

"Sure, like when your tummy gets all"—Lucas wriggled his fingers around in a distinctly wormlike manner over his belly—"and you get scared even though there's nothing to be scared about. And when it happens, I think of my favorite time." He closed his eyes and inhaled deeply. "Smells like my dad drinking his morning coffee."

Bee crossed her arms defensively, coming to a halt. "Well, I don't get scared like that." Which was a complete lie, though for some reason, she said it anyway.

But Lucas kept his eyes closed and the peacefulness that fell across his freckled features was enough that Bee found herself doing the same. The scents of hot ghee and burnt flour and cinnamon perfume floated under her nose. She was back in the safety of Granny's old kitchen after a long day at school, steam coiling from the chapatis puffing up on the stove and an assortment of colorful threads and beads and half-braided bracelets on the table—Granny's latest arts-and-crafts venture. And Bee smiled despite herself.

And then she frowned, because there was a second scent lurking behind the ghee. Her eyes snapped open.

"Here it is."

Lucas gestured to a garage-size shed held together with an assortment of rotten wooden planks and corrugated sheets of metal clearly left over from the construction of outhouses (or as Bee liked to call them, hold-your-breath-for-dear-life-as-you-pee huts).

"The neighborhood storage shed," Lucas said. "We should be able to find everything we need in here for the canoes, and your loon problem, too."

Bee nodded slowly. She should have been glad—a solution to the loons meant she was one step closer to seeing Alina again. *Alina.* Just the thought pushed her forward.

But there was a maddening tickle at the back of her throat, a scratchiness that wouldn't go away no matter how many times she tried to swallow it down. A warm wind blew up the gravel road and past the shed, covering them in a light dust that prickled the eyes and stuck to the skin. And making the scent grow stronger. No, this definitely wasn't in her head.

Bee choked down the smell as Lucas tugged the door wide open, and she finally placed it. The distinct scent of gingerbread—and it smelled a lot like danger.

· 11 ·

A Crumb Is Found

Bee didn't want to step one baby toe into that shed. The pungent smell coiled into her hair, sticking to her skin. It was the same awful feeling that had wrapped itself around her the second she had first set eyes on the rusted old bike abandoned by the side of the gravel road.

"You good?" Lucas asked, raising a red eyebrow. "I told you there was something weird about this place. We don't have to go in if you don't want to."

It was one thing to admit you were creeped out to an old friend like Kitty, with whom Bee had a fantastic history of exchanging creepy happenings. It was a whole other thing admitting it to the goggle-sporting, ghost-believing Lucas. So Bee only spent a few seconds gathering her nerves before she gritted her teeth.

"I'm good."

Then, against her better judgment, she followed him inside.

The scent that had brought a chill to Bee's spine was softening now, or maybe she was getting used to it—like the stench of trash on garbage day—allowing the distinct aroma of mold and dust to shine through. Lucas flicked on the light, revealing a space much larger than the exterior suggested and piled from floor to cobwebbed ceiling with labeled plastic containers and cardboard boxes held together by duct tape. Dead moths littered the cement floor, and what might have been the yellow eyes of rodents peered at her from the darker corners. And there were *a lot* of dark corners.

Bee wove her way between the towers of boxes, passing piles of tires and broken shovels and enough gardening supplies for a small town. There didn't seem to be an end to the space, as if the walls themselves had given up trying to keep all the junk inside and simply melted into the shadows.

"Why do people keep storing their stuff in here?" Bee opened up a box, finding it loaded with printer paper and dried-up art supplies. "It must be impossible to find anything."

Somewhere a rodent squeaked, and Albus hopped off Lucas's shoulders and bolted toward the sound.

"True." Lucas grabbed a role of duct tape from an open container labeled "circus." Bee dearly hoped that wasn't his solution to the leaky canoes. "But it's more fun that way. Once, Mom sent me up here to see if I could find an old typewriter, and I spent a whole day just wandering around and picking up neat stuff—"

"What about something on loons?" Bee cut him off. "Have you ever seen like a nature book or information pamphlet? Or better yet," she muttered under her breath, spotting a discarded router, "do you know where we can get Wi-Fi?"

"Right, your loon problem." Lucas lifted a hand to stroke Albus, who was still off chasing rats somewhere, and when his hand found only air he adjusted his blue swim goggles instead. "What's your problem, exactly? Loons are pretty shy, and I've never heard of them bothering people." He snapped his fingers abruptly. "Oh! Are they pooping on your dock?"

Bee nodded, feigning interest as Lucas launched into a detailed description of how he'd once fought off a battalion of seagulls intent on "redecorating" his mother's writing studio window—the one that overlooked the lake. Should she tell him about the loons that seemed to be gatekeeping the passage to the abandoned lot? Should she share with Lucas that the loons were actually probably most certainly the canoe saboteurs that had been plaguing the cottaging community, and that they were taking directions from none other than a witch?

Maybe not.

"Yup." Bee nodded the second Lucas finished his

speech. "It's definitely loon poop on the dock. So anyways, I'm going to look this way for something useful, and maybe you can look somewhere over there." She pointed to the opposite end of the shed, and then, before Lucas had the chance to respond, plunged deeper into the maze of boxes.

It was annoying how *intense* Lucas got about everything, turning even a dumb story about cleaning bird poop into an epic adventure. Bee briefly wondered where he got his knack for storytelling, but mostly she wondered how come he never seemed to feel embarrassed about anything. Ever. Even when he really should.

A flash of Albus's orange fur caught her eye, and her unease about being alone in the shed won out over her dislike of cats. She followed, squeezing between two shelving units stacked with grass seed, narrowly avoiding a long pair of rusted hedge clippers perched precariously next to a line of empty jars, until the edge of her elbow caught something.

A few loose sheets of paper fluttered to the ground, their edges tattered like they'd been ripped out of a diary or journal or something. Bee wasn't going to bother picking them up, given the state of things—no one was going to notice a little extra mess. But the burning sensation on her elbow where the pages had grazed her skin made her stop. That, and the same scratchiness in her throat.

Suddenly, the shed felt much quieter. Bee swallowed

and crouched to the floor, fingers hovering over the paper. She was only vaguely aware of Albus nearby, watching closely as her eyes prickled, blurring the edges of her vision. And then it was everywhere—that overwhelming scent of danger. Bee's breath quickened and her legs tensed, and it was all she could do not to run away as fast as she could. But she didn't.

Maybe it was the cat's judgmental stare, or maybe it was Alina's penchant for trouble rubbing off on her. But there was something going on here, and Bee couldn't help but wonder, *What would Betsy Chillers do?* Certainly not run away with her tail between her legs. Certainly not before taking a peek. Plus, what if this had something to do with that awful witch? Bee took a trembling breath and grasped the pages.

For my new friend. And then the darkness lurking in the corners of the shed rushed forward.

The first thing Bee noticed was the rocking motion and the breeze across the nape of her neck. It was a breeze that could only come off the calm surface of a lake in the early morning. She blinked as the red edges of the canoe came into view, and then the paddle's smooth handle in her hands. Bee's breath hitched as she took in the familiar surroundings of Storm Lake. Somehow, she wasn't in the shed anymore.

Bee gazed out at the tree line across the lake—at the Gladers' cottage and then at Lucas's family's cottage next door—and frowned. Was it just her, or were the pines slightly shorter? And where was the Gladers' trampoline? All the while, Bee continued to paddle, and it occurred to her that she was paddling rather hard. The rhythmic splash and creak of the canoe was almost frantic.

Sweat beaded her temple despite the cool breeze, and she felt herself turning to glance over her shoulder, pulse quickening. That was when she caught sight of her reflection in the lake's surface, so quick she barely had the chance to register it. But there was no mistaking it. Her frizzy hair and thick-rimmed glasses were gone. Instead, she was looking at a lanky boy with shaggy blond bangs clutching the canoe paddle as though it might bite him. On his shirt there was a large logo emblazoned below the words "(Something Something) Farm"—it was difficult to read with the frantic paddling. Then her heartbeat—no, his heartbeat—reached epic drumbeat levels as he turned and fixed his gaze on the property across the lake: the abandoned lot. He was scared. But of what?

A second later, the canoe tipped.

Panic flared as water rushed into her open mouth and black feathers speckled with white flashed before her eyes. The canoe was flipping upside down!

The last thing Bee saw was a green spiral-bound diary slipping out from under the canoe seat, and her hand reaching out and catching it before it hit the water.

Then the boat's hull fell over the top of Bee's head, encapsulating her in an echo chamber that blocked out all light. And nearby, the eerie call of loons rang over and over again, as though they were jeering.

What the heck was that? Bee's eyes snapped open as the vision crumbled away. She was back in the shed, sitting on the floor with the loose pages in her lap. Her clothes were dry as a bone, and there was no sign of the boy anywhere. The panic that had grabbed hold of her earlier was receding, like a wet patch drying on the dock under the hot sun. She shook her head, turning her attention back to the pages—pages that must have been attached to the green spiral-bound diary at some point. The first side was a study of loons, sketched in charcoal that smudged on her fingers. Some had wings outstretched, others were floating quietly, and there was even one captured in mid-dive. Whoever drew these was clearly obsessed. Obsessed or . . . She looked closely at a tiny word scribbled on the bottom of the page in crooked letters and her breath hitched as she deciphered the letters.

Stay away.

She recalled the panic as the canoe flipped, and the loons that were clearly chasing the boy. And the green diary. Could it be that he had the same problem she did? Bee flipped to the next set of sketches of a few more loons drawn in the same charcoal, but these were close-ups of their sharp beaks, circled around and around several times. She pursed her lips. Dangerous indeed!

Albus's deep purr pierced her thoughts, and Bee quickly folded the pages, tucking them away into her cargo shorts.

"Sorry, couldn't find anything on loons," Lucas grumbled as he walked up to her, then flashed a toothy smile. "But I did find these!" He dangled a purple pair of swimming goggles in the air, chest puffed a bit too proudly. "Now we can go swimming together."

Bee tried hard not to groan as she followed Lucas back outside. Under normal circumstances, she would have shut down the whole swimming thing ASAP. But she was too preoccupied to protest, her thoughts circling back to what she'd just experienced. To the lake that hadn't quite felt the same as the lake she knew, as though the vision was from a long time ago. To the young boy in the canoe, and how she could feel every terrified beat of his heart as though it were her own. And most of all, to the revelation that she wasn't the only one who was wary of the loons.

She gritted her teeth, her thumb running over the braid of her bracelet. Maybe this wasn't the first time strange things had happened on Storm Lake. Maybe this had all happened before.

· 12 ·

A Sip of Chai for Sleepless Nights

"How much further?" Bee asked, ignoring the bits of gravel bouncing into her sandals.

The forest pressed in on either side of them, thick and dark and full of whispers. But Bee kept her eyes on Lucas's polo shirt and Albus's fuzzy red tail swinging like a grandfather clock's pendulum down his back. She was warm—too warm—but for some reason didn't want to take off her long-sleeve shirt, as though it were offering some protection.

Lucas was walking fast, turning the corner ahead and disappearing in the foliage. Bee's pulse quickened, and she jogged to catch up, rounding the corner . . . Lucas was nowhere to be seen. Cold sweat ran down Bee's back and her pulse drummed in her ears. *Where did he go? Why did he leave me?*

The forest of scaly trunks and emerald moss quivered in her peripheral, and it almost looked like eyes blinking. Bee squinted, trying to spot his red hair. The gravel path stretched out in front of her in a long gray line, curving up at the end in a steep climb. She could see down at least a kilometer or two.

And then a figure appeared, long and spidery, detaching itself from the woods and stepping onto the path a few feet away from her. Bee's breath caught on a sudden whiff of gingerbread, but there was nowhere to run. Her chest squeezed as she backed away, but there was nowhere to hide. Nowhere to escape.

Bee woke up with a start, sitting straight up in bed. She'd meant to stay awake past her parents' bedtime and sneak out to the dock to meet Alina—Lucas had managed to "fix" the holes in both canoes with duct tape—but a heavy rain had decided to settle over Storm Lake. It was the kind of storm that one sees coming from far away, where the rain starts slowly and builds to a steady, even drumming against the windowpanes. It was night now, and still storming, without any sign of a break. Bee's heavy quilt was thrown to the side and the bedsheets were damp from sweat. Something had woken her, but it wasn't the storm, and already her dream was fading. Bee shivered as though the cold from outside were seeping into her bones.

It was only a nightmare.

What she needed was a warm cup of milk. Or better yet, a warm glass of chai. It was something her mom had started to do for her own sleep troubles: keeping a small batch of decaffeinated chai in the fridge to soothe the mind on sleepless nights. Bee tiptoed barefoot across the laminated floors, passing her parents' bedroom and then Granny's, with its door ajar.

It took only a minute to locate the thermos in the fridge, and a minute more to heat it in the microwave (Bee stopped the microwave timer right before the *beep* so she wouldn't wake anyone). She took a sip, the cinnamon notes and rich sweetness instantly warming her belly and chasing away any remnants of the nightmare.

Much better, she thought, wrapping herself in a fuzzy blanket and taking a seat on the living room couch. It was comfortable here, perfectly situated to watch the rain drip down from the terrace overhanging the deck and patter over the lake. As her eyes adjusted to the dark, Bee glanced back toward the bedrooms, from which a soft snore rose every so often. Granny always kept her door open so that she would have some light in case she woke up at night. But as soon as Bee approached, the snoring stopped. She looked in and traced the faint outline of the bedpost and checkered quilt, the stacked pillows . . .

That's odd. Bee frowned as she peered through the dark, scanning the single bed as best she could. It was hard to tell, but it almost looked like . . . Her ears tingled uncomfortably and she drew her thumb over her braided bracelet. Granny's bed was not only empty, but untouched, the sheets undisturbed, as though no one had ever slept beneath them. Which of course wasn't possible. Bee started to step forward for a closer look, her hand on the bedroom door, but then stopped herself. *This is ridiculous, I'm just tired. I'm not seeing things right.*

But her frown remained as Bee turned back to the lake. Just in time to see the mysterious flicker of light dancing in the abandoned lot.

• 13 •

A Welcome Visit on a Rainy Day

Bee woke the next morning to the same steady thrum of rain and the pungent smell of freshly made peach pickle. A blanket of gray hovered over the lake and a humid chill hung in the air. It stayed this way through a quiet family breakfast of brown sugar oatmeal, and a few hours of flipping through old nature magazines and a single copy of a Havoc Boys book Bee had found in the Gladers' game cabinet. It was amusing, but certainly not Betsy Chillers.

Bee sighed, wondering what Kitty was up to with her new friends and hoping she wouldn't forget about her by the time Bee returned from cottage country. After all, Kitty was known for making friends quickly and dropping them just as fast. *That wouldn't happen to me, though, would it?*

Bee sighed again as she realized she'd read a full page from the Havoc Boys book but was so distracted she couldn't remember a single word.

Before she knew it, the morning had slipped into afternoon teatime. Though for Granny and Mrs. Bakshi, who were chai lovers, teatime was pretty much all the time. They couldn't get enough of it, from the lingering deep aroma to the spiced creaminess to the feeling of the piping hot mug against their fingers. There was a chai for every occasion.

"Are you sure you want to sit outside?" Bee asked, peeking over her book. Her gaze inevitably caught on the gigantic pyramid of jarred peach pickle on the kitchen table, prepared by her mom the night before, and she did her best to ignore it. "Looks like that big storm they were calling for finally arrived, so it's going to be wet."

Her dad's voice rose up from somewhere deep inside the cottage. "Oh, this isn't the *real* storm, trust me. You would have heard the loons call before it started— they're the call-up-a-storm birds, remember?"

Bee didn't respond, trying not to roll her eyes. She really wasn't in the mood for impromptu nature factoids, and especially wasn't in the mood to hear about loons.

"I want to watch the rain from outside," Granny insisted, pointing to the approximate location of the

Adirondack chairs sheltering under the terrace.

Bee knew better than to argue with her grandmother. She put down her book. "All right, then." She got up, handing Granny a throw blanket. "At least bring this."

No sooner had Granny settled outside with her steaming mug and blanket than Bee's dad sprang into action, disappearing into the back bedrooms and returning with a large box.

"What's all this?" Bee leaned forward as he deposited the box on the coffee table.

There were bags of white and gold balloons, stacks of ribbon and curlicue decorations, matching plates and napkins and fun party hats . . . *Granny's party!* Bee's heart sank a little.

"I thought you could make a card," he said, going back to the rooms and bringing out a large white piece of cardboard, which had been folded in half to form one gigantic card, big enough for even Granny to read.

"Why does it have to be so big?" Bee asked, briefly bringing a hand to her bracelet.

"You need a big card for big feelings." Her dad raised his bushy eyebrows. "And something tells me you've had a lot of those lately."

Bee made sure she was turned away from her dad before rolling her eyes. But because she was stuck inside the cottage and there wasn't much else to do on a rainy day without Wi-Fi, she grabbed a bunch of colorful markers and Scotch tape and scissors and laid it all out on the living room floor. Bee traced the beginning of a flower, then stopped, then started again, then stopped. What should she draw? What should she write?

The pit in Bee's stomach was back, and without meaning to, she found her gaze drawn away from the card and toward the window and the curtain of rain—toward the lake and the abandoned lot waiting on the other side. And Alina. Her stomach rumbled in response and she patted it, surprised. She couldn't be hungry, not yet. But seeing the lot made her feel empty, like she was desperately missing something . . .

Mrs. Bakshi came over from the reading chair, gave Bee's dad a light peck on the cheek, and joined him in the blowing up of a gazillion balloons.

"You know, I never managed to surprise your grandmother," she said excitedly. "She was always sharp as a whip. But she had to be, raising three girls on her own in a strange new country. When we arrived in Canada, I was only seven. And I was the eldest! She was a remarkable woman."

Bee's heart sank a little more and she put the marker down. Her parents didn't know she never gave out the invitations so there wouldn't *be* much of a surprise. They continued to laugh and joke about Granny in the good ol' days (whatever that meant), but Bee was no longer listening. She didn't want to be there. In fact, she wanted to be as far away from her parents and the cottage and Granny's party as possible.

Bee stared at the card in front of her, watching as a line of tiny black ants wove their way around her foot, over a pair of crafting scissors, and under the coffee table with a few granules of sugar. Bee picked up the scissors, brushing off the ants, and was resisting the urge to run the sharp metal edges right through the middle of the card when familiar dark eyes pressed themselves against the porch window.

Alina! Bee startled, accidently nicking the inside of her thumb with the scissors. A single bead of blood swelled, and she bit her lip to stop a small yelp from escaping. Her parents didn't seem to notice a thing.

Alina motioned to her, with her wolfish grin and billowy pirate shirt that had somehow managed to stay dry. And suddenly the dark cloud that had circled Bee's head lifted (life was always more delightful when punctuated by unexpected welcome visits) and she grinned back.

"That's looking wonderful!" her mom remarked just as Bee decided to forgo the frills of the card and got up. "Oh, where are you going?"

"Just on the porch, hanging out with . . ." Bee stopped herself. Alina had asked her not to say anything, in case the witch overheard. Still, it didn't feel quite so nice having to keep their friendship a secret. She stepped over the impressive mound of white and gold balloons, pinching her thumb even though it had already stopped bleeding. It felt almost like crossing her fingers against a lie. "I'm going to sit outside," she said, as the cottage phone began to ring.

From inside, the sound of the rain was like white noise, constant and staticky. But outside, when you really stopped to listen, the layers of sound began to separate like buttery flakes of pastry—the drum of the downpour on the roof, the droplets falling from the leaves and trees, the rivulets streaming down the grass, the drizzle over the lake.

The screen door creaked shut and Bee pulled her polo on over her head as the humidity washed over her. She moved the second chair to the far edge of the porch for Alina.

"I thought you didn't like exploring around here," Bee teased as Alina took a seat and then slid over for Bee to join. There was just enough room for them both.

"I don't," Alina said, swinging her legs out and wriggling her toes, showcasing that she was still barefoot. "This is more of a checkup mission."

"A checkup for what?" Bee asked.

Alina snuggled into the side of Bee's polo, as though they'd known each other forever and Bee was *hers* somehow. It didn't bug Bee, though; in fact, she felt her shoulders relax and her brow smooth and the strange emptiness in her belly fill with warmth.

"Checking up on you, silly!" Alina said. "You didn't show up the other night and I got nervous for some reason. Nervous that you didn't have it in you and got too scared of your parents to meet me on the dock." She turned, fixing Bee with those dark eyes and lowering her voice to a whisper that was almost swept away by the rain sounds. "Nervous that the witch got to you."

"The witch won't get me. I'm being careful," Bee assured her, then frowned, because ever since she met Alina, it had felt as though something—or someone— was watching her from between the pine trees. And then there were the horrible dreams, always filled with the scent of gingerbread. Was that how it started? Her chest tightened.

But then Alina smiled, and Bee's fears drip-dripped away like the rain.

Alina reached her hand up and twisted a finger around one of Bee's loose strands of frizz. "I thought your hair was a bit too wild before, but I've decided I like it."

It was the kind of thing Kitty would say, but Bee never really believed her. The frizz and Bee were in a never-ending battle, and Bee would never be content. But for some reason, it was easier to believe things when Alina said them.

Bee turned away, patting down the frizz hurriedly. "That makes one of us."

A cool breeze brushed her left side as Alina peeled away, standing and stretching her hands up. Then she skipped toward the stairs, laying her hand gently on Granny's before jumping down onto the grass.

"Don't forget tonight. And thank you, Bee," she said. "For taking care of that awful loon problem. I knew I could count on you."

Loon problem? Right, the loon problem! She'd been so caught up with thinking about her next meeting with Alina, she had completely forgotten she was supposed to get rid of the loons. Especially since those loon sketches in the storage shed had been a dead end. The truth was, she had no idea what to do.

"Wait!" Bee called out to Alina, jumping up.

She was hoping the visit would last a bit longer, but maybe she shouldn't have been surprised—it was exactly the type of thing Alina would do, and already the rain and the forest had gobbled her image up. In the corner of her vision, she caught the sparkle of handlebar streamers where the bike leaned up against the back porch as though waiting for her. Bee swallowed nervously.

"Lucas just called," Granny said, then yawned and took a long sip of her now cold tea.

"What?" Bee asked, grateful for the distraction. "How did you know that?"

But she simply closed her eyes, as though pretending to go back to sleep.

A moment later, Bee's dad stuck his head out. "My, that pickle is strong. It's enough to make even a bird's eyes water!" He chuckled. "That's funny, you see, because most birds don't have a sense of smell." He paused, waiting for a reaction that didn't come. "Yeesh, tough crowd today. Anyways, Lucas wants to know if you want to go over to his place to watch a movie."

Bee didn't have to think twice about it. She shook her head. "No thanks."

"Are you sure?" he asked. "Apparently Hanna will be making poutine or something. I believe it involves a lot of melted cheese."

Bee sighed, watching the infinite ripples and dimples of the rain on the lake. This didn't sound like an activity that Alina would partake in. Knowing her, she was probably already heading back to the abandoned lot, or hiding out in some equally fantastic tree house in the woods. The pit in Bee's stomach was gone for now, but she knew it was only a matter of time before Alina's sweet words and soothing presence melted away into rumbling emptiness once again.

"No, I'm . . ." She paused. "I'm not feeling well."

"Oh no, really? Well, you could always invite him back here, if you want?" her dad suggested.

Bee grimaced. Why wasn't he taking the hint? "With that peach pickle stinking up the whole house? No way, the spice is going to burn his nostrils off."

Her dad froze in the doorway, and Bee froze as she realized what she'd just said. She didn't dare turn to look at him.

After a long pause, he cleared his throat. "Is that any way to talk about your mom's cooking?" The reprimand sounded off coming from him, unpracticed. After all, Bee wasn't the kind of kid who talked back. And if she did slip up once in a while, she was always quick to apologize.

Maybe it was because she'd just seen Alina, and Alina made her feel different. Maybe it was because the bike was putting her on edge. But this time, Bee didn't say anything. Finally, the door creaked shut, and Granny opened her eyes again. *How cheeky! She's only pretending!*

"How did you know about the phone call?" Bee asked.

Granny raised a white eyebrow. "A better question is, why did you use that tone with your father? And don't you want to go over to see Lucas? He's a nice boy."

"Lucas?" Bee slouched low in the Adirondack chair. "Lucas is . . . unusual. Especially with the goggles and the cat he carries around." *Unusual like I used to be, before Kitty.*

"Ah yes, he's not like other kids, that's for certain." Granny took another sip of chai, her hands shaky. "But isn't that what makes us wonderful? We're all a bit different and a bit weird. Beauty is not in the face; beauty is the light in the heart."

Bee crossed her arms. "You mean 'different' like Dad and his fun facts?"

"I admit your dad's fun facts can grow tiresome." Granny chuckled. "But he shares them because he's excited about all the new things he's learned since going back to school. His family didn't have the money when he was younger, and sharing knowledge is his way of sharing his joy."

"And Mom? And her cooking? And . . . bargaining? Ugh, it can be so embarrassing."

"That is my fault." Granny smiled. "When she was your age, I had to be careful with money. Waste not, want not. It's important not to take anything for granted. Your mom is trying to teach you that."

Bee crossed her arms. It didn't fix the fact that she wasn't allowed to have brand-name clothes even when everyone else was wearing them. Or that her hand-me-downs were always a tad too baggy. But as Kitty liked to point out, *If anyone can pull off vintage, it's you* (was that a compliment? Bee could never be sure). And it certainly didn't make up for her parents stopping her from going to the Betsy Chillers amusement park just because *they* didn't get it.

They sat in silence, listening to the chorus of the rain as the spicy scent of peach pickle wafted out from the screen door. Spicy enough to keep the mosquitoes at bay. Or make a bird's eyes water.

Wait a second. Her dad said most birds didn't have a sense of smell, but what about magic birds controlled by a witch? What if the mysterious sketches from the diary weren't just a warning about how dangerous the loons were, but also about how to stop them? Bee's eyes lit up as an idea sparked. *The circles around the beak weren't about their hole-in-canoe-poking sharpness, but the nostrils!*

Granny began to hum softly, her voice disappearing into the drip of the rain, and Bee wondered briefly whether she'd tattle about Bee's evening plans to her parents. Bee wiggled her fingers together anxiously. Probably not, but still . . .

"Granny?" Bee turned toward the other Adirondack chair and stopped, her eyebrows pulling together.

A chill ran up her spine. There was a mug of chai on the overturned peach crate beside her, but it was cold and untouched. A blanket, now soggy from the rain, lay folded next to it. And though Bee could have sworn she'd heard Granny's soft humming a second before, the chair was empty.

· 14 ·

Exploring in the Dark

This time, Bee was prepared. She said her good nights early and then waited patiently in bed, listening to the sounds of her parents brushing their teeth and closing their bedroom door for the night. Then she waited a little while longer, fully clothed in dark leggings and an oversize hoodie under the blankets (and recently doused in bug repellant), watching as every second the sky darkened further and more stars winked into existence. And then, finally, it was time.

Quick as a hummingbird and quiet as a whisper, Bee rolled out of bed and crouched down, retrieving one of her mother's precious jars of peach pickle, which she'd stashed there earlier. The glass shone and the pickles flashed like jewels in the moonlight. Bee lifted her window up wide, unhooked the window screen, and wriggled herself out onto the front deck (she certainly wasn't going to risk that creaking screen door again). Flashlight and pickle in hand, she stole down the lawn, still wet from the earlier rain, and onto the dock, where the canoe waited silently among the cattails.

Three loons were settled in the canoe, two on the seats and the third on the center wooden yoke. Six red eyes fixed on Bee at once. *This can't be normal loon behavior.* She shuddered, unscrewing the jar lid and wondering how this was really going to work. If the loons really were sensitive to strong smells, there wasn't anything more spicy than Indian pickle. But there was still a niggle of doubt in Bee's mind.

The loons swayed, shaking their beaks and ruffling their wings. The spicy tang of the peaches hovered in the air. Bee stepped forward, holding the jar toward them.

"Get off my canoe! Shoo!" she said.

The loon closest to her slid off the bow and plopped into the water, followed closely by the other two. Bee breathed out with relief and shook out an oily glob of pickle onto the stern of the canoe. She did the same on the bow for good measure and then shook out a couple more globs onto the dock. Bee placed the now half-empty jar on the dock, amazed as the loons watched from a safe distance. *It actually worked!* She'd fulfilled her promise. Now all that was left to do was wait for Alina to show up.

Bee zipped up her life jacket and lifted the paddle from the bottom of the canoe. *If she shows up.*

A few weeks back, when Kitty found out that there were signed copies of the first Betsy Chillers at their local bookstore, they had made plans to bike there after school. Which was complicated for Bee, because her parents didn't really like it when her hobbies—especially inappropriately spooky hobbies—cut into family dinnertime. But after a lot of promising that it was a one-time thing and she wouldn't buy anything (Bee could still be excited and fawn over Kitty's copy), her mom agreed. So Bee waited for Kitty after school, until the first text came in.

> Hey, something came up, I'll meet you at
> the bookstore. XO

And that was fine, because Kitty knew lots of people at school and probably didn't want to be impolite and rush off without chatting. But after twenty minutes of wandering the aisles of the bookstore, Bee started to feel self-conscious of the clerks' stares—probably wondering whether she was going to buy something or not—and her stomach was growling from the dinner she was missing, and there was still no sign of Kitty.

And then the second text came in.

> Hey, so sorry I know you were really looking forward to this, but something else came up. Let's get the signed copy another time.

The shallow water sloshed under the canoe. What if the same thing happened with Alina? The trees on the property creaked as worry built up in her head. What if Alina suddenly realized there were better things to do than hang out with someone like Bee?

Abruptly, the doubt crumbled away like a loaf of stale bread. *She* had arrived, a pale figure stepping out from behind the marsh.

"Ready?" Alina asked, her teeth white in the moon's light. Her curls framed her delicate features like curtains of ink.

"Ready," Bee said, trying not to smile too widely.

Alina glided to the bow and perched on the front seat. Bee pushed away from the dock with the paddle, plunging it deep into the water. She breathed out slowly, nervously. If Bee was afraid of the lake water in the daytime, night was a hundred times worse. The stars were reflected in its black surface—a magical view from shore, but slicing forward through the water, it felt as though it was a trick, a pretty distraction from the unknown that lay beneath the surface.

A loon's howl rolled over the lake, and Bee looked

back to find the silhouettes of the three loons trailing them from a safe distance.

"They won't bother us," Alina said from the front. She stuck a finger into the pulpy glob of pickle on the bow. "Your spicy solution seems to have worked. I knew I could count on you."

Alina's words gave Bee courage. The canoe pushed forward, and it felt as though they were moving faster than before. The duct tape on the bottom of the canoe held fast. Soon the white branches poking out of the water came into view and Bee stopped paddling, letting momentum carry them the rest of the way. The bow gave a small thud as it touched land.

"We made it," Bee said to herself, half in awe.

Alina skipped out of the canoe and tied it loosely to the nearest cedar, as Bee made her way out and ducked under the line of trees. And bumped into the wrought-iron patio set she'd noticed before.

"Ouch!"

A cloud was passing over the moon, temporarily blocking its light, and Bee flicked on her handy flashlight. The pine needles and leaves that had previously carpeted the cobblestone path were gone, freshly swept to reveal the soft grays of polished stone sunk deep into cement. She frowned as the circle of light landed on a single-serving iron teapot and empty mug sitting in the center of the small patio table. *These weren't here before, were they?*

"Alina, did you do this?"

What a kind surprise, a tea party at midnight! Bee reached out, gasping as her fingers made contact with the teapot's hot surface, and lifted the lid. The aroma of freshly brewed chai escaped. Bee hiccuped with delight, lifting the teapot and pouring its contents into the mug. And then she drank.

It was the best chai she'd ever tasted, the cream thick and the sweetness deep, balancing perfectly against the masala blend. Better even than her mom's chai. Before she knew it, the cup was empty and her stomach gurgled. She needed more.

Bee shook her head at the wonder of it, sweeping the flashlight over the property. The overgrown grass that filled the old tires was gone—instead, freshly planted blueberry bushes spilled out from the rubber centers. The dead grass and clumps of weeds had been raked out—weeks of hard work that seemed to have occurred over a day or two. Bee's breath hitched as she stepped forward. Even the sandstone retaining wall had a distinctly less crumbly appearance, as though someone had taken great care in patching up the holes and straightening out the leaning sections.

"Alina?" Bee called again, but she must have gone ahead, because there wasn't a soul in sight.

The wind shifted and the clouds moved, letting through the moon's light again and showcasing the most beautiful transformation of all. Thick vines now wound themselves around the rickety archway above the steps leading through the sandstone wall, studded with bouquets of lush roses in full bloom, their petals ruffled like twirling frilly dresses. Bee walked through in awe, inhaling the sweet perfume deeply.

And yet it was nothing compared to what lay ahead. Gone were the skeletal ruins and piles of debris. Vanished were the cracked slabs of marble and pool of water collecting in the house's foundation. Instead of the remains of the abandoned house, a handsome beige building of stone and intricate brown wood paneling waited at the top of the sloped grassy hill. It looked like something out of a fairy tale—with its pretty scalloped roof and front-facing balcony and gingerbread window trim. The same rose vines climbed the trellises that leaned on either side of the front door.

I must be dreaming. But she could still taste the sweetness of the chai on her tongue, and before she knew it, Bee found herself standing in front of the door, watching as a flicker of light passed behind its oval of frosted glass. Hesitantly, she reached out, the cool brass handle sending a shiver up her arm. The door swung open.

Instantly, a warm glow pooled out from all the windows in the cottage.

"Aren't you going to come in?" Alina asked.

She stood in the entryway with a small gas lantern swinging from her hand.

"What is this place?" Bee breathed, stepping over the threshold into a large entryway of deep burgundy with gold edging. Any illusions as to this being all a "nice gesture" from Alina had vanished. This was something else. Something impossibly wonderful. But she still had to ask. "Did *you* do all this?"

Alina grinned and placed the lantern on a side bench next to a familiar pair of shoes and a folded checkered shirt. She extended a hand toward Bee. She was warm, her skin so smooth it didn't feel like skin at all. Bee let herself be guided down a long hallway covered in framed watercolors of wildflowers and delicate-looking leaves and cedars crisscrossing over patches of glittering lake.

"No, it's not me. I'm amazing, but I'm not magic." Alina paused, her smile wavering and her eyebrows arched as though waiting for Bee to object. "The house does this all on its own. I discovered it a while ago, but I didn't think you'd believe me unless you saw for yourself."

Bee took a deep breath, but it didn't stop the shakiness in her voice. "I believe you."

"But you haven't seen anything yet."

She followed Alina up a wide stairwell, marveling at the beauty of the knots and wavy lines in the stairs' wood grain until they reached the top. Alina pushed a door open and Bee gasped. It was like being back in the forest, with silver maples stretching high into a ceiling of blue and trilliums carpeting the four corners of the room. Except it was the forest on the world's most perfect night, with stars giving off a light almost as warm and bright as the sun, a refreshing breeze, and no mosquitoes in sight. Bee walked through the room, brushing her hands against the very real trunks, following the branches.

Oh! Her finger hitched on something and her eyes caught a flash of color. Bee angled her head, and there it was again. She couldn't see it at first, but the closer she got, the more the trees and branches meshed together to form bookshelves, rows upon rows of them that stretched as high as the trees, filled top to bottom with books.

And they weren't just any books.

"The Betsy Chillers series," she breathed, picking out a favorite. Instantly, a rumble passed through the white trillium flowers and their dark green leaves in the far corner, which grew and reshaped themselves into a soft, flowery lounge chair. "You're a fan as well?"

"No, *you're* a fan—I guess the house picked up on that. Showing off." Alina smiled, and Bee couldn't help but smile back.

She continued to scan the titles. They were indeed all Betsy Chillers, mixed in with a few nature magazines, of course—a library curated to her taste—until her eye found something different. A green spiral-bound diary, with a slightly warped spine and old water splotches. *That's odd. Is it here by mistake?* Bee tried to tear her gaze away, but she couldn't. It was as though the diary was calling to her, trying to tell her something. Had she seen it somewhere before? Bee reached a hand up and then stopped as Alina grabbed her arm. She was suddenly much closer than expected, and Bee jumped back, startled.

"For someone who likes spooky, you scare easily." Alina's teasing words were as light and sweet as powdered sugar. She took Bee's hand. "Come on, there's so much more to see."

Alina led her to the top floor and up a thick wooden ladder into the cottage attic. Except instead of a dusty room, Bee found herself popping up into a massive tree house kitchen stocked full of lilac macarons and fancy candies. Carefully, she peered over the ledge of an open window into the evening sky and the emerald green of the treetops below.

"Incredible!" she gasped, as Alina handed her a peppermint chocolate. The thin chocolate coating melted on her fingertips as she bit it in half. It tasted way better than Kitty's party favors. "How?"

Alina smiled, spinning away back to the cabinets in search of other sweets. "Because it's what you want. And this house will give you everything you've ever wanted."

Bee nodded thoughtfully. *The entire Betsy Chillers collection, "normal" party foods, a break from my family . . .*

"So these are all the things *I* wish I had. What is it that *you* want?" Bee stopped herself, cheeks warming. Asking Alina what she wanted was insinuating that there was something missing in her life. Something that wasn't perfect.

Alina turned to face Bee, shrugging. "The house has already given me what I want. Tonight is about you."

And before Bee could respond, Alina grabbed her hand, leading her to their next destination—a ceiling-high wardrobe filled with row upon row of never-before-worn clothes. Cute skirts and cutoff tops and (tastefully) torn jeans and as many summer dresses as Bee could ever wish for.

The next few hours flew by in a dreamy haze. It was like someone had built a house just for Bee, someone who knew her perfectly and wanted her to be happy and wanted her to stay forever. Alina was right.

Bee flopped onto a cushioned chesterfield in the living room, admiring the new outfit Alina had picked out for her in the never-ending closet of wonders: a sapphire-blue romper that undulated and waved with the smallest of movements, like ripples on the lake. And the best thing about it: It wasn't a hand-me-down from her cousin.

Although the short sleeves are a bit chilly. Bee looked around for a throw blanket, and immediately the large marble fireplace at the room's heart roared to life. The orange-and-pink flames licked the air, covering Bee in a warm hug.

"This house is magical," she squealed. "I love it here."

Alina sprawled out on a sky-blue sofa with carved lions' paws for feet, her hair splayed over the armrest. "When you're here, you don't have to worry about your parents or feel bad about wanting friends that get you. Here you can change who you are—really change—and fit in. There's nowhere better."

Bee pulled at a lock of her frizzy hair. "Well, I can't change everything."

But Alina only grinned in response, so Bee got to her feet to inspect the mantelpiece. There were so many small treasures and unexpected miracles in this place, it was difficult to sit still for long: pastel vases filled with dried flowers, wooden bowls of potpourri, some kind of silver bell that looked like it had come off a bike, a single picture frame.

Bee brushed off the thin layer of dust over the frame. It was a picture of Alina and some other, equally pretty girl, standing side by side and beaming. The girl was really wonderful; her dark eyes gleaming fiercely. In short, the total opposite of Bee. And it looked as though the girls in the photo were standing in this very living room, with the blue couch and the chesterfield in the background.

"Who is that?" Bee asked, sensing Alina coming up behind her.

She couldn't help the twinge of jealousy in her stomach, even though she knew that wasn't fair. Alina could have other friends—in fact, someone as cool as her probably had loads of other friends, all much better company than Bee. Friends without weird parents or funny food or . . .

Alina wrapped her arm around Bee's shoulders. "See for yourself."

Bee looked up above the fireplace, where a long mirror shimmered into existence. There was Alina, looking like her usual wonderful self. And there was that girl again, wearing a sapphire-blue dress, with clear skin and no glasses and silky-smooth hair tied up in a pony. Bee gasped, reaching up to touch her face. The girl in the mirror reached up, too.

"I'm . . . I'm . . ." Bee couldn't find the words.

For the first time in her life, she actually looked like someone.

Someone who might belong in Kitty's clique. Someone who had cool parents and went on trips to the Betsy Chillers amusement park. Someone who wasn't just the new brown girl in school who Kitty happened to take swimming lessons with.

"Perfect," Alina finished for her, and Bee's thoughts were enveloped in a rush of sweetness that was better than all the lilac macarons and peppermint chocolates in the world. "It's everything you've ever wanted."

· 15 ·

Run, Run, Run, as Fast as You Can

T he morning walk with Granny was filled with the chorus of excited tweets from the forest's winged inhabitants—from the cooing of mourning doves to the jingle of robins—as they tucked into a meal of earthworms left wriggling on the gravel path from yesterday's rain.

"Another puddle, Granny, big step," Bee said, holding on to her arm and navigating around the minefield of water.

Granny laughed. "I'm too old for this. I'm pretty sure I'm in my eighties, or even nineties, you know." She tilted her head to the side. "Why do you always drag me out on these walks, anyway? I'm a much better napper than walker."

"Walking is good for you," Bee chided, feeling the soft braided bracelet tickle her wrist.

Soon the sun would be out again, and with the forecast calling for a hot and steamy day, the forest floor would dry up in no time.

"But I'm so tired, and I feel a nap coming on." Granny gave an exaggerated yawn and then blinked innocently.

Bee was no match for Granny when she truly wanted something. "Fine, you win."

Anyhow, she was much too busy reliving her night to care for long walks in soggy socks and sandals. Her night at the abandoned lot, which in fact was not abandoned at all. It was *magic*. Bee lifted her face to the sun, recalling the warmth of the fireplace and how difficult it had been to say goodbye for the night. And Alina's warning.

A cloud temporarily threw her into shadow.

"Whenever you want to come back, just meet me on the dock after dark," Alina had whispered. "I'll be there. Or . . ." Her dark eyes widened. "You could stay, you know. There's an extra bedroom just for you. The one with the balcony. It's safer that way, too."

"Safer?"

Alina had leaned closer, and even though there were no windows nearby, a cold wind had brushed Bee's fingertips.

"The witch is watching you. I can sense it. She's

going to make her move soon."

Bee's throat had tightened. "Her move?"

Alina hadn't responded, letting Bee steep in the chill that had enveloped her body.

But witch or no witch, Bee couldn't stay. Her parents didn't know where she was. She had left in the dead of night, without asking permission. If they woke up to her missing in the morning, Bee was sure that they would never let her out of their sight again! And the thought of that was almost as scary as an encounter with the Gingerbread Witch herself. Almost.

No, she didn't stay overnight. Not this time, anyway. While Alina watched from the water's edge, camouflaged behind the ghostly white branches sticking out of the dark shoreline, Bee canoed back across the lake, docked the canoe without any loon incidents, and slipped back through the window into bed.

A few hours later, when the sunrise tickled her eyelids and she turned on her side for a few more minutes of warmth cocooned under the quilt, it could have all been a dream. A wonderful, beautiful dream full of sweet roses and peppermint chocolate and enchanted libraries and the coolest friend one could ever ask for.

Maybe it was a dream. But when Bee finally rolled out of bed, the sapphire-blue romper had rippled around her torso and legs.

And that's what she thought about now, clothed in her drab brown capris and a touch-of-sparkle

T-shirt (she couldn't possibly have worn that romper in public—Kitty would never approve of its lack of bling) as she helped Granny back into the house. Bee was ready to slip her sandals off and perhaps laze about for a while in her room to inspect the magical outfit—she might even join Granny in taking a nap—when a certain goggle-wearing, cat-carrying kid stepped out of the cottage.

His wild red hair seemed extra wild today, with Albus nestled around his neck with her eyes firmly shut. A fresh stain (probably orange juice or iced tea) speck-led the front of his matching red golf shirt.

"Your parents let me in," he stuttered, realizing Bee's confusion. "I came over to see you and they were about to head out for a swim. Said I could wait inside until you got back."

That sounds like them. On a beautiful morning after a long day cooped up inside the house, her parents would probably spend the whole day by the water. What wasn't cool was letting Lucas inside so he could ambush her with his weirdness. It had only been a few hours, but Bee was already missing Alina's magic house—especially the part about no parents and no Lucas.

"So what's up?" Bee asked, keeping her sandals on as Lucas joined her outside. She walked toward the gravel path, hoping to lead Lucas back to his own home. There was way too much on her mind to keep company with him today, and for some reason she found his presence was a tad more annoying than usual.

"I came over to see if you were all right," he explained, reaching up reflexively to pet Albus.

"Why wouldn't I be all right?"

They reached the gravel path. Lucas stopped, his cheeks turning a bright pink.

"I called to see if you wanted to come hang out yesterday," he said, "and your dad said you didn't feel well."

"What? I'm not—"

Right, the call. Bee grimaced, remembering how dismissive she'd been when her dad had asked her about going over to the neighbors'.

"You weren't really feeling sick, were you." Lucas slumped his shoulders.

"No," Bee said slowly. "But it's not because I didn't want to see you. It's because I was busy!"

Okay, so it wasn't a complete lie. Bee *had* been busy chatting with Alina, and then she *had* been busy looking forward to visiting the house across the lake.

"Oh, I guess that makes sense." Lucas cheered up to his usual excitable demeanor and adjusted his goggles. "Busy with what? Is it something I can help with?"

He really was quite persistent. Almost . . . desperate. Bee sighed. "Not that it's really your business, but I was hanging out with—"

She stopped abruptly, aware of a shift in the forest.

The birds weren't singing, and a cool breeze lifted the hairs from her neck, bringing with it a peculiar scent.

Gingerbread.

Goose bumps ran up the skin of Bee's arms, and instinctively she held her breath, too, listening just as the rest of the forest was. Waiting . . .

"You were hanging out with . . . ?" Lucas raised an eyebrow, oblivious to what was going on.

Couldn't he feel it? Couldn't he sense it? Pools of shadows seemed to seep into the earlier sunshine and Bee clenched her teeth, bringing a thumb to her braided bracelet. But it did little to ease her nerves.

And then, around the curve of the path ahead, a figure detached itself from the trees.

"Lucas, run!"

The forest was breathing again, the birds chirping and the leaves rustling, but Bee couldn't hear beyond her breath. Blood pounded in her ears and puddles splashed up her ankles as she sprinted down the path in the opposite direction.

The Gingerbread Witch had finally decided to pay her a visit—just as Alina had predicted.

"Bee!" Lucas gasped, not far behind. "What's going on? What's wrong?"

Bee risked a glance back, past Lucas and a terrified Albus, hanging on to his shoulders for dear life. She couldn't see anything, as though the witch had disappeared, and that only made her run faster.

"I'll explain after," Bee said between breaths, thinking furiously.

The cottage country maze of gravel paths was made up of loops upon loops upon loops. If the witch knew her way around, which she likely did, she was probably taking a detour in hopes of cutting them off ahead. Which meant that to escape, they needed to be unpredictable. They needed to get off the gravel path.

"This way," Bee yelled, turning hard right onto the thin dirt trail she'd spotted earlier.

Instantly wet leaves were slapping her in the face and arms, the edges of twigs and low branches poking her in the chin. Bee brought her arms up to shield her face and kept running, through thickets of mosquitoes and past groves of tall pines, until her sandals were veritable blocks of mud and the front of her shirt was soaked through with rainwater and sweat.

Darn! The dirt trail diverged, then abruptly ended. Bee scanned the foliage, noting the mossy facade of a boulder rising about halfway up the trees. And there, pushed up against the boulder, in an impressive makeshift construction of dead logs and canvas tent and birch bark, was something resembling a cabin. Bee didn't have time to think—she made a beeline to it, ignoring the beginnings of a stitch in her side.

"In here," she gasped to Lucas, pushing open the plank of wood that acted as a door and flinging herself inside.

For a shelter in the middle of the woods, it was spacious enough, completely closed off to the elements with a half circle of plexiglass above their heads to let in some light. Bee found a large bag of old grass seed and slumped onto it. With her breathing no longer ragged and her pulse slowing, she could finally take in the details of their hiding spot. Although there wasn't enough room to stand, whoever had built this place had had comfort in mind. Layers of old carpet padded the earthy ground, colorful fabric had been hung against the stone wall in places like tiny prayer flags, and the heavy canvas camouflaged most of the branches holding the whole place together.

"What the heck was that about?" Lucas asked, wide-eyed and trembling almost as much as Albus.

He removed her claws from his shirt and cradled the poor cat against his chest. Dead leaves and spiderwebs and all kinds of other debris stuck out of his hair, and his knees and hands were covered in mud where he must have taken a slip. Bee wiped the dirt and sweat from her forehead, shuddering at the thought of what her own hair might look like.

"You wouldn't believe me even if I told you," Bee said. And that *was* the truth.

Lucas located a lumpy pillow and took a seat across from her.

"We're friends, aren't we? Course I'll believe you."

Friends? Bee hadn't even told Kitty about this yet,

and the thought of keeping something from her best friend made her stomach queasy. But it wasn't so much the creepy-lady-hunting-them-through-the-forest part—it was the part about Alina. Kitty made new friends all the time, but Bee couldn't help but feel she wouldn't be very happy to find out about the cool, pretty girl living in a magic house.

But here Lucas was, stuck hiding in the middle of the forest with Bee. She'd already dragged him into this.

"There's a witch," Bee said slowly, watching for the curled lip of a sneer or eye roll that was sure to follow. Lucas stayed dead still. "There's a witch that catches children."

His eyes behind the goggles grew wide and his face turned so pale, even the constellation of freckles seemed to dim, like tiny red stars going out.

"Should we tell our parents?" he asked, his lower lip trembling.

He definitely believed her.

"No," Bee said quickly. "Maybe. I don't know. There's a lot of things I haven't been telling my parents about lately. There's a lot I think they wouldn't understand."

Lucas seemed to consider this. "You mean, more things like the witch?"

"Kind of." She wasn't planning on telling him about it, but the words came out on their own. "There's this cottage, this house across the lake. Everyone thinks it's abandoned, but it isn't. At night, it comes . . . alive. With magic! Incredible magic."

Lucas's eyes were growing so wide behind his goggles, Bee wasn't sure how much more he could take. But he didn't interrupt, and she didn't stop. "The first time I went to the abandoned lot it was because I didn't want to deliver these party invitations, you see, for Granny's party. I feel bad about that, lying to my parents. But I'm glad I went across the lake. And I went there again last night. I think you have to go after dark or else it doesn't work."

Bee paused to catch her breath. There, she had finally let them go, all those secrets that had been piling up. Albus was calming down, too, and settled back around Lucas's neck. She let out several deep purrs, blinking her human eyes slowly.

"Do you believe me?" Bee asked nervously. "Aren't you going to say something? I'm sure you have questions . . ."

By now Kitty would have interrupted her about ten million times, asking for more details, wanting to cross-examine the evidence. And even then, she would have feigned skepticism in front of anyone else—*Bee, are you sure that's what happened?*

But not Lucas. He shook his head and rubbed his hands over his arms vigorously, as though breaking out of a trance.

"I believe you. Sometimes if I stare too long at that

place across the lake, I get the heebie-jeebies. It's hard to explain." He frowned. "But going across the lake by yourself isn't safe. That's water safety one-oh-one. You should have told me sooner. I would have gone with you."

Bee smiled with relief. Of course Lucas would focus on the annoying, not-at-all-important parts of her story. He was all right with witches lurking about, but canoeing solo was not okay. *Also, who says heebie-jeebies?*

"Don't worry, I wasn't alone," Bee said. "I've been with Alina this whole time. She's the one who showed me all about the magic house in the first place. Your sister is way too cool. You could learn a thing or two from her."

Lucas nodded thoughtfully, then grew very still.

"Are you okay?" Bee asked, reaching out. Her fingers grazed his hand, startling him.

"Sorry, I'm fine." He frowned. "It's just that . . . Bee, I don't have a sister."

· 16 ·

A Teeny-Tiny Lie

Bee felt the little shelter tilt and placed her head in her hands, squeezing her eyes shut and willing the world to stop spinning. How could Alina *not* be his sister? Who was she, then? Why would she lie? *It doesn't make sense.* Didn't Lucas's mom, Hanna, mention Alina that time they came over for dinner? Then again, Lucas had mentioned that that was Albus's nickname.

Bee groaned at the knot in her stomach, which was made worse by Lucas's hand on her shoulder and Albus's furry face on her forehead. She wanted to be left alone. She gritted her teeth, ready to head out the door, but instead she remained seated on the sack of grass seed as her eyes scanned the front of the shelter. Her pulse quickened and an itchiness was building in her throat. The kind of itchiness that told her to run. And at the same time, told her there was something here that needed investigating. *What would Betsy Chillers do?*

Bee took several deep breaths. Slowly, her pulse returned to normal, and her mind calmed down enough for her to start noticing the details of their hideout. Like the bits of string tied to an assortment of pressed flowers, each one strung from the ceiling and flashing vivid crimsons and fuchsias like dried gems, as though the owner had taken great time to make things pretty. Along the far wall, some of the stone was exposed, peppered with grooves stuffed with rolls of parchment and crayons. The light shifted from the plexiglass above, and for the first time she saw the tattered paper sign tacked to the canvas wall.

"'Clubhouse,'" Bee read out loud as the scent of danger curled under her nose. Her jaw tensed unconsciously.

"What is it?" Lucas asked, his voice suddenly quiet and small, as though he, too, sensed a change in the air. Even the fur along Albus's spine was raised in a strip. "Are you getting that feeling, you know, like you did back in the shed? Because I'm getting a real weird vibe."

It surprised Bee that Lucas had paid such close attention to things.

"Yeah, I guess I am," she muttered.

In fact, it was the exact same feeling, which was both terrifying (the memory of plunging into the lake was the opposite of fun) and also good. The diary pages had turned out to be a huge help with the loons. Which meant somewhere in this clubhouse was another clue, and this time, it might have something to do with the witch.

Lucas attempted to calm Albus down with cuddles, or maybe he was trying to calm himself down, while Bee crawled toward the pile of pillows. She moved them to the side one by one, searching for the source of the chill crawling up her spine.

"Did you say something?" Bee asked.

"What?"

She bit her lip, turning away from the pillows and toward one of the holes in the stone wall, where the light didn't quite reach. It was faint but unmistakable, a circling whisper that was too soft to make out.

"I think there's something in here," Bee said, trying to keep the quaver from her words. She crawled toward the hole—a hole just big enough for a child's hand to pass through—and gingerly squeezed her fingers inside. It was deeper than expected. The cold of the stone was smooth at first, but soon gave way to cold, squishy forms wriggling across her skin. "Gross."

Bee was up to her elbow now, the squishy forms pressing against her arm, and then finally her fingers grazed something else. She took a breath and quickly pulled her hand back, watching in disgust as the fat forms of yellow caterpillars spilled over the carpet.

"This must be it." She held the object up for Lucas to see. It was a candle stub, the wax frozen in cream-colored drips and drops, the wick blackened and short.

"What do we do with it?" he asked as Albus leaped from his arms.

Bee opened her mouth to answer, but already a memory was whisking her away from the yellow caterpillars inching over her sandals, from the clubhouse and its hanging pressed flowers, and from Lucas's concerned gaze as he removed his goggles for the first time since they'd met.

The candle flickered in front of her, illuminating a cobblestone path. It was a cloudy night with the moon hiding somewhere behind the tall pines. Bee could feel the hug of overalls around her hips, and from the tightness at the base of her skull and the rhythmic brushing between her shoulder blades, a thick braid of hair. This wasn't the boy from her first vision who fell into the lake. This was another kid, a girl. And judging by the tight curl of her fists, she was about to do something difficult.

Ahead was a wrought-iron table with two chairs, surrounded by a well-kept lawn and a few tires filled with wildflowers. The same kind of flowers as the dried ones in the clubhouse. Bee felt a jolt as she recognized the abandoned lot, and then a second jolt as the girl sat down and placed the flickering candle in the center of the table. Because sitting across from her, with her

150

billowing blouse and large ringlets and eyes as big as saucers, was none other than Alina.

"You came," Alina said, something tugging at the corner of her lips. "Last time you left in such a rush . . ."

"Well, you surprised me," the girl answered. Her voice was strong and a bit deeper than expected. It was the voice of a kid who wasn't afraid of anything, or was pretending not to be.

Alina cocked her head to the side, a single ringlet brushing the table. Shadows danced across her features, making it difficult to know whether she was smiling or baring her teeth. "I thought you liked surprises. Isn't that why you asked me to teach you my tricks?"

Tricks? What tricks? A pang of jealousy reverberated in Bee's belly as she took in the friendship between these two. But the strain in the girl's posture, the curtness of her tone, told her whatever friendship existed was about to come to an abrupt end.

"You've gone too far this time, and I won't be coming back." The girl was speaking faster now, as though time was running out. "You need to stop this, Alina. Stop this or else—"

Alina's jaw opened slowly, hanging slightly lower than any normal jaw should. And then her eyes creased and she began to laugh—an eerie, high-pitched laugh that covered Bee's arms in goose bumps.

"I'm leaving now." The girl pushed back her chair and grasped the candle. "I hope you're happy."

Somehow, this made Alina laugh even harder. The girl's heart was beating wildly and it took everything she had not to run. Instead, she kept her composure and began walking as fast as possible back down the cobblestone path. Alina's laugh echoed behind her. But what was so funny? Bee wished she could turn back, wished she could stay with Alina a bit longer, but the girl kept walking and never looked back.

She was too scared.

Bee pushed herself off the carpet, where she was lying down next to Lucas, the candle between them. Slowly, he blinked his eyes open.

"Was that . . . *her*?" he asked, and Bee's neck prickled uncomfortably. "Alina is terrifying, how can you stand her?"

Bee swallowed. All right, so the memory didn't paint Alina in the best of lights, but that didn't mean anything. She didn't like the way Lucas was talking about her. Whether she was his sister or not didn't mean anything. *I'm sure she had her reasons for not telling me the whole truth. I'm sure there's a reason for whatever that girl was accusing her of.*

Still, Bee couldn't help but wonder what that was all about. What was the memory trying to show her? And who was that girl? Slowly, she pocketed the candle stub.

The walk back along the trail and up the gravel path was a long one. At least, it felt long to Bee, who had

152

to listen to a million and one of Lucas's theories about Alina, the mysterious girl who apparently haunted Storm Lake.

"She's definitely dangerous," he said. "Did you feel the way that other girl was scared? You don't have to worry about things by yourself anymore. We'll get to the bottom of this together, you'll see."

I'm not worried, Bee thought with a frown. She didn't like how easily Lucas had decided Alina was a danger, seemingly forgetting all about the witch who was baking children in her oven. *She's not a bad person just for one teeny-tiny lie.* After all, wasn't it normal to keep some things to yourself, even from your best friend? Surely if everyone was completely honest and acted like themselves 100 percent of the time, they'd have *no* friends, just like . . . Bee glanced at Lucas. *If I could just talk to Alina . . .*

"You and me, solving a mystery like paranormal detectives." Lucas adjusted his goggles back over his eyes and grinned as they parted ways, Albus coiled snugly around his neck. "Maybe I'll even get to see a ghost!"

That night, Bee waited until her parents were in their beds snoring before climbing out the window and tiptoeing to the dock. She was getting really good at sneaking out, and she wasn't sure if that was a good thing anymore. Bee quickly pushed the thought from her mind.

The moon was bright, the sky cloudless, the stars

reflected in a perfect mirror lake. Bee sat at the edge of the dock and brought her knees in. She forgot to bring a sweater, and there was a chill over the water. Three loons swam lazily in the center of the lake, somehow knowing Bee was in no mood for them tonight.

I'm sure Alina is a nice person. She's a good friend. Bee cupped her hands around her mouth. *"Alina!"* she called in a half whisper. She couldn't risk any louder than that.

One of the loons looked her way briefly before plunging underwater. Other than that, there was no movement, no sign. Crickets sang and toads croaked, and Alina didn't come. Eventually, Bee resigned herself to the fact that it was time to go to bed.

She went the long way this time, risking the creak of the screen door in favor of a cup of microwaved chai. It was like holding a hug between her hands, and she needed that right now. Except it didn't taste as sweet as she remembered, and the spices felt off, and Bee found herself yearning for that creamy magic chai she had drunk across the lake. The chai that had seemed to have been waiting for her her whole life. The chai that was maybe even waiting for her now. With a sigh, she poured the leftovers down the sink drain.

Bee was so tired and upset that by the time she tip-toed by Granny's open bedroom door to climb into bed, she didn't even notice that someone very important to her appeared to have gone for a midnight stroll as well.

· 17 ·

Bee Goes Back

The Bakshi family was having egg paratha for breakfast—a cottage meal favorite, it seemed. And as always, it was delicious, from the round, flaky, butter-flavored pastry to the slightly runny egg yolk and cracked salt. But not as delicious as Bee remembered. There was something off about the food, and despite polishing her plate clean, a strange hunger remained grumbling like a beast from the depths of her stomach.

Bee's brows were angled and her foot tapped the ground and her mouth puckered as though she'd just bitten into a lemon wedge.

Alina hadn't shown herself last night on the dock, but there was surely a good explanation. Maybe she'd gotten held up at home, wherever that was. Maybe she'd been too tired to explore?

The only way to find out for sure is to go over and ask her. The lake was a clear baby blue this morning, inviting. Lucas would be angry with her—he'd already told her that she shouldn't go back.

"It's dangerous, Bee. Please." His eyes had been the eyes of someone who worried too much, like her parents, and his fiery hair had practically glowed as the sun hit it through the leaves. "Promise you won't go back alone."

"I promise," Bee had said. But it had been a lie.

The pit in her stomach was growing again, and the mystery around Alina made Bee want—no, need—to see her even more. She wanted to feel the way she had when Alina cuddled up to her that day in the rain, she wanted to feel the way she had when Alina grabbed her hand as she showed her around the magic house. Bee wanted to be that girl in the mirror above the mantelpiece. That wasn't something Lucas could ever understand.

Bee brought her dishes to the sink. She would have to head out soon since Lucas had a bad habit of popping out of the woods right after her walks with Granny. Fortunately, luck was on Bee's side today.

"I'm so tired," Granny complained as soon as Bee made mention of the morning walk. "I'm in my seventies, or was it nineties? Anyways, I want to go back to bed for a bit. *Please.*"

"But walking is good for you, keeps you strong."

Bee crossed her arms and then smiled. "All right, you win again. Maybe I'll bring you for a walk this afternoon instead."

Granny smiled. "Nap time!" she said gleefully and shuffled back to bed.

Mr. Bakshi rubbed his hands together as Mrs. Bakshi started the dishes. "Bee, can you help me out? It's for the party."

Bee's neck prickled and she slid out of her chair to bring her dishes to the kitchen.

"We're trying to figure out the seating," he continued, raising his bushy eyebrows. "Do you remember how many of our neighbors were free to come?"

It felt like a weight was being lowered onto her chest, the weight of a lie. *You don't have to feel bad—remember what Alina said*. But it was easier said than done.

"Even a rough idea would be helpful," her mom said. "So I know how much to cook. And speaking of delicious food, did you take one of my peach pickle jars?"

Bee's ears tingled uncomfortably at the thought of the pickle globs resting on the canoe at that very moment—evidence she'd completely forgotten to clean up. It was for a good cause, though! And why were her parents like this, always insisting on pushing their food onto everyone? Always involving Bee in their party plans against her will?

"Why would I take a jar of pickles?" The words burst out of her mouth before she could stop them.

"Not everyone is as obsessed with them as you are."

"Excuse me, obsessed?" Her mom blinked several times. "You know it's your Granny's special recipe, and I thought you liked—"

"Well, I don't." Bee hurried toward the door for her sandals, her ears burning so hot she worried they might fall off. "Things change, you know. I don't like the same things as before. I'm not a little kid."

Bee didn't dare glance back—she couldn't believe what she'd done, and already the guilt was seeping into her thoughts. But there was another feeling, too, a thrill that coursed through her veins like a sugar rush. By the time Bee was outside, the weight lifted completely.

It was early enough that a few drops of dew still clung to the grass and the wooden planks of the dock were a shade darker from being wet. The canoe slid easily out of the cattails and Bee didn't hesitate as she used the paddle to climb inside and push off the dock.

Alina will tell me what's going on, Bee thought as she pulled the water back and pushed the canoe forward with each stroke. *I'm going to get to the bottom of this.* Most cottagers would still be sleeping at this time—what was cottaging for, if not to wake up late to a cup of sweet tea and stretch lazy mornings out into relaxing afternoons?

The tremolo laughter of a nearby loon echoed around the lake as Bee docked on the shore of the abandoned lot, but when she turned to scour the lake, there was nothing to see.

Bee shook off her life jacket and took a deep breath, a resolute breath. Then she marched under the cedars and along the leaf-covered cobblestones and past the rickety archway and up the crumbling steps. There was no more garden, no more flowers, no more magic. The house was back to its dilapidated, half-standing former state. There was no grand doorway or scalloped roof. The fireplace iron grating swung on its single hinge and looked like it hadn't held a flame in decades.

Bee picked through the splintered wood and cracked stone and dust-covered everything, making her way to the small pool of water in the kitchen. Where she'd dipped her feet in the water and where she first met Alina.

Bee cupped her hands around her mouth. There was no need to be quiet this time.

"*Alinaaaa!*"

Her voice bounced off the remnants of the stone walls, snaking around the tree saplings, rushing over the moss floors. Even though Bee wasn't scared, there was a troublesome knot in her stomach and a lump in her throat.

The trees stayed silent as she scanned the darker parts, peering past the trunks. *Alina will come.* Black-capped chickadees, merry specks of brown and black, flittered around the debris before moving on to more sheltered areas. The stately shape of a great blue heron with wings outstretched glided overhead before landing in the nearby marsh. Its daggerlike beak—used to impale fish—glistened in the sun, reminding her of the long clippers in the neighborhood storage shed.

But Bee wasn't going to give up on Alina so quickly. She studied the rubble to pass time, trying to picture how all the million little pieces of the house could come together at night. There were a few chips of the burgundy paint, and was that a picture frame? Something led Bee to inspect the fireplace, running her hands over what was left of the mantel until her thumb touched something cool.

She stopped, retrieving the small silver bell, her heart beating a bit faster suddenly. It was a bike bell. Completely intact. Bee felt the compulsion to check over her shoulder.

Don't be silly. There's nothing dangerous here. The witch is on the other side of the lake.

But Bee couldn't shake the uncomfortable feeling that someone was watching. She turned the bell over in her hand, enthralled by its mirrorlike surface, and rang it. The tone bounced around the rubble like a high-pitched sigh.

This wasn't just any bike bell. She wasn't sure exactly how it worked, but like the diary pages she'd found in the storage shed and the candle from the clubhouse, there was a memory attached to this bell. A memory that might help Bee uncover a bit more about the past. She could tell from the tightness in her chest and the unpleasant scent that clung to its shiny exterior. *But how do I activate it?* The other memories had simply . . . happened. She rubbed her thumb over it and waited. And waited.

Nothing.

With a sigh, Bee tucked the bell into her pants pocket, just as a dry snap sounded to her right—branches cracking under a weight—followed by a small cloud of black-capped chickadees taking flight. Bee's heart suddenly leaped into her throat. Maybe she could talk to Alina another time.

She made her way toward the front door, making sure to step on the safe moss. Another dry snap sounded directly in front of her. Bee froze. A chill filled the air as a cloud crossed the sky, and she didn't have to see anything to know—she wasn't alone.

Betsy Chillers's first rule of thumb: Never dismiss a chill.

Heart drumming, Bee hopped back toward the kitchen, hoping to get out that way instead. The pines took on a dark shade of green, and it seemed as though night came early. Shadows grew under the debris, seeping out from the fireplace, pooling out from the rickety stairs. Was it her imagination, or did a shadow flicker around the crooked sink? Bee leaped forward onto the broken marble slab, then jumped again, aiming for the top of the exposed stone wall. From there it would be a quick jog down the hill to the steps, a sprint along the cobblestone path. It would only take a second to untie the canoe and push off into the lake.

Bee didn't make it to the lake, though. On her second jump, her foot slid in her sandal, losing its grip on the smooth marble surface.

"Ahh!" Bee yelped as her ankle bent the wrong way and her hands smashed hard into the floor tiles.

So much for my brilliant escape plan. But it could have been worse. Her hand was okay, save for a tiny scrape, and her ankle only throbbed a little bit, which made her think it was a light sprain. Still, it made it very difficult to run. Bee hobbled to her feet, grasping a long, dead branch for support, and shuffled back toward the doorless entrance, ignoring the urge to speed up too much.

Thankfully, there were no other ominous snaps, and Bee was able to shuffle all the way down to the water's edge. Trembling, she didn't even bother putting on her life jacket. She climbed into the canoe and pushed off in one swift motion.

It wasn't until she was halfway across the lake that Bee paused to look back. The cedars swayed slightly, covering up any sign of the old building, blending seamlessly into the shoreline.

Why did I get so spooked? Bee wondered, shaking her head and checking on her ankle. It didn't look hurt, but there was an uncomfortable twinge. All right, so it was a bad sprain, then. Maybe Lucas's paranoia about Alina was getting to her. The clouds moved past the sun, chasing the shadows away as the lake turned back to its usual turquoise.

At least her trip hadn't been completely in vain. Bee patted her pocket, making sure the bell was still there. Soon, they'd be able to find out what the girl in the memory was so afraid of (something told Bee it had nothing to do with Alina and everything to do with a certain children-baking, forest-dwelling scary old lady).

And then, as Bee took a last look at the pale, dead branches, the pungent stench of the marsh on the air, the horizon began to tilt as the canoe capsized.

The paddle was swept from her grip.

The life jacket was thrown from the bow.

The last thing Bee heard before the canoe tipped over and she was plunged underwater was the loons' call, echoing over and over and over again.

· 18 ·

Chura to Share

Bee was a good swimmer, a strong swimmer, Granny would say when bragging about her granddaughter to friends, but strength didn't matter when you were afraid.

The cold water shocked the breath from Bee's lungs as it enveloped her. The bell was long gone, but that was the least of her concerns right then. She squeezed her eyes firmly shut, forcing her arms into movement, kicking her legs despite the twinge in her ankle. Her heart hammered in her ears.

Scientists had come a long way in identifying every creepy-crawly breathing thing that existed on land. The oceans and waterways, however, those were a different story. Something bumped against her foot and Bee squealed, letting out a stream of precious oxygen. She wasn't sure which way was up anymore. She was too scared to open her eyes, too scared to look.

Was this how the boy with the shaggy blond hair had felt in the memory? With a grimace, Bee realized she wasn't sure how that memory had ended. Did the boy make it out okay? Or was he still down there in the lake?

And then, as her last breath slipped out in a stream of bubbles, something cold wrapped around her arm. Bee broke the surface, gasping, and felt the slippery life jacket being pushed under her. *Alina came! Of course she came.* The water moved, rippling away from her body as she was dragged forward. Her ears filled with rushing, bubbling water.

Bee didn't dare open her eyes until she felt the metal ladder of the dock under her hand and the hard plastic step under her foot. She'd made it. Her breath slowed as she swayed there, half-submerged in the lake water, her heart thudding back into its normal rhythm. Her throat burned.

"Thank you," she gasped, wiping the water from her eyes and looking up. *Time to set things right with Alina. I'm sure she has a good explanation!* Except what Bee saw didn't make sense in the least.

"Gingersnaps!" a gravelly voice responded, and Bee nearly let go of the ladder. "You birds need to work on your rescuing. You got me soaked!"

The witch stood on the dock, shaking the water from her shoes. Her face was a sliver of white between her long brown locks (now that Bee was so close, they were more of a dark reddish color) and the long brown coat.

She began putting her shoes back on, but paused as Bee caught her eye. "I can't take all the credit here. It was a team effort."

The witch nodded toward the water, and it was then that Bee noticed them. The three loons paddled around her, their feathers glossy and their black bills sharp. What was the witch implying—that the loons had *saved* her? Bee gasped, unsure whether to leap onto the dock to get away from their red eyes or fall back into the water to get away from the witch.

"Well, I can tell you're in no state to chat." The witch grinned, showcasing a missing front tooth. Something moved amid the knotted locks of her hair, something that resembled a beetle. "Come see me when you're ready."

Bee tried to summon her courage; she even opened her mouth to say, *There's no way I'm ever going to visit you!* But no sound came out, and the witch was already walking off the dock, leaving behind the spiced aroma of gingerbread. And there, resting in a small puddle beside the ladder, was the bike bell.

"Binita!" her mom called as she rushed down the hill in her lemon-bright Kerala with a fluffy towel in hand.

"Are you okay, darling? What happened? I thought I heard something and when I looked up through the window, there was a canoe flipped over in the middle of the lake!"

Right, the canoe. Bee glanced back to see that the loons or the witch or someone had managed to bring it back to shore, tucking it far enough into the cattails that it wouldn't float away. And then she remembered what she'd said to her mom the last time they spoke.

"I'm fine, I'm fine," Bee muttered, looking down.

But it was as though their fight about the missing pickle jar had never happened. Her mom merely wrapped her in a towel and lifted her out of the water, straight into a bear hug. "Sweetie, you're freezing," she fretted. "At least let me prepare you a snack while you change. Something spicy to warm you up."

Food did sound nice right about now. Bee stepped forward on her sore ankle and winced.

"Yes, thank you," she said, camouflaging a groan.

Bee really didn't feel up to explaining to her mom how she'd hurt her ankle. So she did her best to shuffle up the lawn with even steps, tucking the bell back into her pocket.

"Wait here, I'll bring you another towel." Bee's mom shut the screen door firmly. "I don't want you dripping water over the Gladers' nice floors."

"Yes, Mom." Bee sighed as she lowered herself into an Adirondack chair, getting comfortable. The lake looked perfectly serene. It was hard to believe that a few moments ago, she had been fighting for breath. "Mom, about earlier . . ."

"We'll talk about that later. For now, you just rest."

Bee bit her lip and nodded. Maybe she'd been too harsh before. Maybe she should apologize now and get it over with. Instead, Bee swallowed hard, and the apology that was on the tip of her tongue disappeared. "You wouldn't happen to know who was on the dock just now, would you? Because there was this lady . . ."

Mrs. Bakshi popped back through the door with enough towels to dry off a boatload of wet kittens. "A lady on the dock, you say? I didn't see anyone. Did she help you? Oh, I must thank her!"

"No, no, never mind." Bee hurried to correct herself. "It was no one."

"Are you sure? What do you mean, was there a lady or not?" Her mom frowned, and Bee thought she caught a flicker of annoyance. Or was it concern? "Anyway, is there anything else I can get you? I'm about to head out for a walk with your dad. He finally finished fixing up that bike!"

Bee closed her eyes. What she really needed right now was a minute to process the fact that the loons, who were supposed to be the witch's feathered henchmen, appeared to have both flipped her canoe and then saved her from drowning. Bee shuddered, and she wasn't sure if it was because she'd narrowly escaped the Gingerbread Witch, or because she was completely soaked, or because her ankle was throbbing gently, or all of the above.

"Actually," Bee said, "could you maybe pass me the cottage phone?"

Bee dipped her hand into the chura—that crunchy, salty, spiced snack made of puffed rice and lentils and fried bits of dough. It was a big bowl or, as her mom said with a knowing smile, a bowl-to-share. It wasn't often that Bee asked if a friend could come over, and even more rare when that friend wasn't Kitty (Bee secretly suspected that her mom didn't care much for her).

Unfortunately, the chura tasted . . . off, somehow. Bee pushed the bowl toward Lucas, her appetite gone, and he unceremoniously smashed a handful of chura into his mouth. Albus carefully watched his hand like a hawk as bits of puffed rice fell from his chin onto the Adirondack chair and the porch. Clearly, he thought it tasted just fine.

"So," Lucas said, leaning back, his lips frowning at the edges. "I'm going to guess that you went anyway."

"How did you know?" Bee asked, belatedly remembering the mountain of towels and overall drowned-rat aesthetic. The tips of her ears warmed from embarrassment. "Right."

"I told you it was dangerous!" he complained, reaching for another handful of chura. "Who knows what could have happened? You're supposed to run away from dangerous things, not toward them—"

Bee held up the bell, choosing to ignore Lucas's erroneous conclusions about her friend. Anyway, it would be easier to simply show him he was wrong. "I think I have our next clue."

Lucas stopped. "A bike bell?"

"Not just any bike bell." Bee shook her head and pushed herself up, hoping her hunch was right. She shuffled toward the bike that leaned against the edge of the porch, the bike her parents had found on their first day in cottage country. The dread that had gripped her the first time she set eyes on it was still present, like a lingering bad smell, but Bee's curiosity had grown stronger than her fear. "I think there's more to this story than we think."

The sound of water splashing reverberated around the lake like ripples; a few cottages down, a group of young kids thundered down their dock. It was an odd sound to have in the background, carefree laughter and splish-splashing under the blue sky. *If only they knew . . .*

Lucas crouched next to her and a piece of puffed rice fell from his chin. He placed a hand on the bike seat. Then slowly, carefully, Bee slipped the bell onto the handle. It was a perfect fit. Then a shudder ran up her arm as the memory whisked her away.

The glittery streamers on the bike's handlebars flew straight back like shooting stars as the girl in overalls zipped down the gravel road. It was difficult to tell in the dim light, but the lake was near, patches of it shimmering between the trees.

The girl stood and leaned forward to meet the hill, pedaling harder than ever as the forest pressed in on either side—thick and dark and full of whispers. Her breath came out in small puffs—there was something in the air that made it difficult to breathe. Sweat dripped off her thick red curls and mosquitoes whined as dusk turned to night. Dark clouds crept over the stars.

She turned the corner, reaching the top of the gravel hill road as it curved back down. The turnoff was close. And then something cold tugged at her handlebars. The bike—gingerbread-brown with a lick of pink icing down its neck—swerved, but she held on tight, her feet pedaling as fast as possible. The faint scent of gingerbread wafted up from her fingers, and she caught a glimpse of cookie dough encrusted like cement under her nails.

The handlebars jerked again, but she squeezed her fingers around them in a vise grip. And now it was obvious—the thickness in the air and the haze floating on the wind. *It's smoke!*

The forest of scaly trunks and emerald moss quivered in her peripheral, and it felt like a hundred eyes were watching her from the darkness. Suddenly, the gravel path seemed to stretch out endlessly, the turnoff gone as if it had never existed. Cold sweat ran down her back, mixing with the ash that fell from the sky, and her pulse drummed in her ears.

The girl held on for dear life as both fear and triumph curdled in the pit of her stomach. It was the kind of feeling that only came when you had done something terrible, the kind of feeling that stayed with you for a long time afterward.

And with a chill, Bee wondered, *What has she done?*

Bee pulled out of the memory first and brought the towels closer around her. The image of the forest crumbled away, but the uneasiness remained. She wasn't sure how long she'd been gone; her clothes were mostly dry from the sun, but a chill remained. A chill deep inside.

"That was intense," Lucas muttered, shaking awake. "I wonder what that was all about, like when the bike jerked to the side as if someone invisible was trying to tip it over. If that girl had been even a fraction slower, who knows what would have happened!"

Bee scowled. "I think you're missing the most important part. That girl did something bad to Alina—I know she did." She crossed her arms.

It was the only explanation that made sense. That girl, whoever she was, didn't appreciate how fortunate she was to be friends with a girl like Alina. How incredibly lucky she was to get invited into that magical house. To be given the chance to be who she truly wanted to be. *Why would anyone give that up?* And for some reason, the horrible events of the past were starting up again and someone was trying to hurt Alina. Except this time, it wasn't some silly girl who didn't understand the true meaning of friendship. This time, it was something much worse.

Bee gritted her teeth. "That witch is after her, Lucas. This is a hunt, plain and simple."

Lucas made his way back toward the bowl of chura, pensive, as Albus swiped at a rogue rice puff. "So you think Alina's in danger?"

"I know she is."

"I guess the only way to know for sure is to talk to this mystery girl." Lucas adjusted his goggles before dipping into the bowl of chura for another crunchy mouthful. "But these memories we're seeing, they clearly happened a long time ago. It's not like we can go out and find her and ask her what happened, right?"

He looked thoughtful for a second, then grabbed the bowl of chura and tipped the remainder into his mouth. Then he took a seat on the upside-down peach crate that was being used as a side table. Bee tilted her head as the orange lettering on its side jumped out at her. *Happy Valley Peaches Farm.* Her eyes lit up. *Happy Valley Peaches Farm! That's it!*

"I guess it's a dead end." Lucas sighed.

Bee carefully laid out the towels to dry in the sun, testing out her ankle. It was feeling much better. And so was she.

"How do you feel about going for a bike ride?"

• 19 •

A Series of Unusual Accidents

Bee stood off her bike seat for better pedaling leverage, her sprained ankle only protesting a bit. Thankfully, it was a small hill, and the bike her dad had fixed up had thick tires that gripped the gravel path with ease. The glittery streamers licked at her hands and her bracelet as she managed to get some speed. And as a bonus, the little bit of wind she created was enough to keep any pesky mosquitoes at bay (as long as she made sure not to leave her mouth hanging open too long on the downhills).

"Are you sure this will be the right guy?" Lucas asked, coming up beside her. "You said his name was Eli?"

How he was able to bike with only one hand while balancing Albus on his shoulder, Bee would never understand. At least with his bike helmet on, the goggles didn't look so out of place.

"I'm telling you, he used to live in your house," she said, sitting back on the seat and reducing the gear. "And he had this look at the market, like he was scared or something, when my mom started talking about the cottage."

And it wasn't simply the look, it was the fact that he had stared directly at Bee for a split second. And there was that warning—*keep off the water*—which made a lot more sense now that she knew he was thrown out of the canoe and into the lake as a kid. Exactly like what happened to Bee.

Of course that wasn't the only reason she knew it was Eli. Bee had finally placed where she had seen the green spiral-bound diary in the magical library. It was the same diary she'd seen Eli grab as his canoe tipped. The same diary from which the pages covered with sketches of loons had been ripped . . . But Bee decided to keep that part to herself. The question wasn't whether Eli had gone to the abandoned house with Alina after dark, it was what had happened next.

As they reached the edge of cottage country, the forest thinned and morphed into a patchwork quilt of farmland. Lucas signaled right with his arm and they turned onto the large gravel shoulder of the road leading into town. Bee was used to biking back home, using the bike path that snaked alongside the city's river to commute to school (she only biked in the warmer months of course, there was no way she was going to bike to school in the snow). Biking in the countryside was a very different experience, though.

The tall buildings and bustling sidewalks and humming cars were replaced with golden fields and lines of oak trees stretching out into a too-big sky. The fumes and honking were replaced with wind rushing over land and the occasional rattle of a car passing by on its way to or from the township of Storm. *Is this what Granny liked about visiting the Gladers?* Bee breathed in deeply and wrinkled her nose. Ah yes, and the sweet aroma of fresh manure, just like the kind her dad used to fertilize the flower garden.

The cows were spread out in the pasture, dots of white against the grassy hills. Bee didn't remember seeing cows when driving by, and biked a little closer toward the fence as she passed to get a better look. Her dad had grown up on a farm, and Bee had heard many stories about getting up before sunrise to tend to the animals (especially when she'd complain about getting up to go to school). But to Bee, seeing cows was nearly as rare as spending a week at a cottage. The bike's tires crunched gravel along the leaning picket fence as she slowed. And then something odd happened.

The handlebars swerved suddenly to the left, as though someone had come up beside her and tugged hard. Bee gasped, pedaling hard to right herself, but no matter what she did, the bike kept jerking to one side.

"Eeee!" Bee yelped as she came crashing down. She rolled sideways, away from the road and into the picket fence, scraping her shins and knees on the gravel.

She sat there, mildly dazed and catching her breath. Beside her, the bike's front wheel continued spinning. *Did I really fall?* Bee wasn't the type to lose her balance while biking, and yet there she was, all dusty and scratched up. It had all happened so fast! A cow mooed in the distance as Lucas screeched to a stop, propping his bike on its kickstand.

"What happened? Did you get a flat?" he asked, crouching beside her. His cheeks were flushed from the ride and spokes of red hair stuck out from one side of his helmet. Albus looked her usual bored self. "One second you were there and the next you were on the ground! Want me to call my mom?"

"No, no, I'm all right," Bee said, picking out gravel where it stuck on her skin.

The whole thing was more surprising than painful, really. It had been as though the bike *couldn't* right itself, as though something was pushing it from the other side.

"Oh no. I didn't bring my phone," Lucas said, checking his pockets.

"Me neither."

Lucas put a finger in the air, eyes wide. "I know, I'll bike ahead for help!"

At the mention of help, Bee's stomach fluttered nervously. It was a good idea: the town was only a five-minute bike ride away, a whole ten minutes closer than the cottage. She could imagine it now: Lucas, in all his goggle glory, dragging half the town back to help. Bee shuddered at the thought. Her hair was an absolute mess, and her hand-me-down clothes were sticky with dust and sweat. *No way*, she thought, pushing herself back up.

Lucas glanced at her legs, and then her foot, chewing his lip. "But you're hurt."

"I can still bike. It looks worse than it is." Bee shuffled back to the bike. "Are you coming?"

Lucas cleared his throat. "I think there might be another problem," he said, pointing to the bike's very flat back tire. "You sure you don't want me to go get help? It won't take long."

Bee ignored the last part. "Oh drats. Well, I guess I can walk."

It wouldn't be easy, of course. But the mild discomfort of her earlier sprained ankle would be worth avoiding the embarrassment of being seen *like this*. Or—and Bee hated to admit it—with Lucas. The faster they got to town and talked to Eli, the faster they could go home. And fast meant fewer eyes on them.

Lucas crossed his arms, the beginnings of a pout shaping his cheeks. "You're trying to do things on your own again. Why don't you want me to help?"

He raised a hand toward an oncoming car, signaling for it to pull over. Blood rushed to Bee's face.

"What are you doing!" She shuffled toward Lucas and pulled his arm down quickly.

The car slowed down momentarily as Bee turned away, ears tingling. Thankfully, it didn't stop. She gritted her teeth.

"I told you, I don't want *that* kind of help! Why can't you just listen?" The words snuck out before she could catch them, and they hung there in the air between them, smellier than the fresh cowpats in the nearby field.

Another car passed by, and suddenly Bee was very aware of how things looked, how *she* looked. It was ridiculous. And embarrassing. She took a deep breath and sighed heavily, hoping Lucas would drop it. She didn't want to fight. She just wanted to get back to the cottage. *I'm not in the mood for this.* But Lucas wasn't the type to notice the obvious.

"Sometimes I feel like you don't even want me around," he mumbled, kicking his bike stand back. "But I know that can't be true because we're friends . . ."

Secret friends! Bee sighed again, biting her tongue. It was exactly the kind of thing Kitty would say.

Thankfully, at that very moment, a large green pickup with large cardboard boxes in the back slowed, and a familiar face popped out the driver's-side window.

"Oi!" the driver said, the truck's taillights glowing

red as he braked and then backed up expertly onto the road's shoulder.

The truck door opened, and a lanky guy with a T-shirt sporting a picture of some old rock band and acid-washed jeans jumped out. He wasn't that scared little kid Bee had seen in the memory anymore, but there was no mistaking the braces and shaggy blond hair, and the "Happy Valley Peaches Farm" baseball cap.

"Eli?" Bee asked. So there *was* such a thing as good luck! With all the accidents she'd had lately, she had been starting to wonder.

"Looks like you got a flat!" he called out, opening the back of the truck. "Need a lift to the cottage turn-off?"

Lucas's expression seemed stuck between relief and irritation, and he looked like he wanted to say something, but Bee didn't give him the chance. She was already crossing the street.

It didn't take long for Eli to pile up their bikes in the back of his truck, and before they knew it, Bee and Lucas were sitting squashed together in the front passenger seat. She leaned as far away from him as she could, which meant their arms were still stuck together with sweat and gravel. *Gross.* At least the peaches Eli had given them gave her something less unpleasant to focus on. Bee bit into the sweetest peach of the summer, savoring every bite as the juices covered her parched throat.

"I make deliveries out of town once a week," Eli explained, "for the folks who aren't as mobile or just too busy to get to the market. What are you guys up to?"

Bee shared a look with Lucas, suddenly unsure of herself. Would Eli remember what had happened ten years ago, or would he laugh at their so-called imagination? She didn't have that much to go on; after all, the pages from the green diary captured a simple moment. But it was a moment that had felt like a close brush with death (and Bee would know, since the same thing had happened to her!). Surely he'd remember. But before Bee could muster up the courage to ask, Lucas was speaking.

"You used to have a cottage on Storm Lake, right?" Lucas asked, cradling Albus in his lap, her tail flicking onto Bee's legs. "Did you ever meet a girl called . . . Alina?"

Eli gripped the steering wheel hard, his braces flashing as he grimaced. "I did. I hung out with a girl by that name for one summer."

Bee noticed his knuckles turning white. "Who was she? Do you know?"

"I was a bit of a loner back then," he said. "Spent a lot of time sketching that abandoned house across the lake. That's where I met her. We were the same age, although she didn't seem to always act like a kid, sneaking out after dark and all. She called herself Alina, but who knows, really." He fell silent.

"Wait, so Alina was a kid ten years ago, and she's still a kid today?" Lucas whispered in Bee's ear with a nudge.

Bee ignored the twinge of unease in her stomach, but that was a good point. If it was indeed the same Alina, how could a girl stay the same age for so long? Then again, how was it possible for an abandoned house to transform into a fantastical paradise each night?

"What was she like?" Bee asked.

"At first?" Eli asked. "Normal. Nice. But when I stopped doing what she wanted . . ." He shuddered. "Accidents started to happen—a slip on the deck here, dropping a glass bowl there—it could have been random."

"Was it?" Lucas asked, eyes wide.

"I don't know." Eli shrugged. "But things kept happening. Once I stopped going to the abandoned house to meet her, I started going for long canoe rides looking for interesting spots to sketch, trees that caught the light funny or turtles sunning themselves on logs. You know, there's so much wildlife around here once you slow down and look."

Bee nodded. As much as she didn't like lake water, she could appreciate how many critters called it home.

"Well, one day I had just finished fixing the canoe— someone had been going around poking holes in the hulls, so weird—so I was a bit preoccupied. And for the first time ever, I forgot my life jacket." He shuddered again. "Of course that was the day it had to happen. I heard something coming up behind me in the water, and then before I knew it, the canoe was tipping. It was so sudden, so surprising."

Lucas inhaled loudly and Bee's neck prickled. "But it was the loons, wasn't it?" she asked. "The loons tipped your canoe, right?"

"I don't know, I didn't see," he said. "Thankfully there was this lady near the dock when it happened. She whistled so loud, and next thing I knew there was a life buoy in my arms. I don't like to think about what would have happened if she hadn't been there." Eli swallowed uneasily. "After that, I realized the best thing to do was keep off the water. And even then, just the sight of the lake . . . Eventually I stopped going anywhere near the lake altogether, and the accidents stopped."

Lucas rolled down the passenger window and they both threw out their peach pits into the beginnings of the forest.

Eli shook his head. "That was all a long time ago, though. Alina would be long gone by now. Grown-up like me, I'd imagine."

So his friendship with Alina didn't end so well. But that didn't mean all those accidents that had happened were because of her. If anything, it sounded like the witch's loons, up to no good.

"You said you did a lot of sketching—did you have

a sketchbook?" Bee took a breath, glancing at Lucas.

"I like to draw, using charcoals mostly." He frowned. "But it wasn't my sketchbook, actually—found it in the attic when I moved in. Some kind of diary, I think. It's hard to remember now. But whoever it was only wrote a few pages."

Bee pursed her lips.

"Hey, you're looking pretty beat up, what's been going on with you?" Eli asked, noticing the remaining gravel stuck to her shin.

Bee grimaced and Eli looked from her to Lucas and back to the road.

"She's been getting into a lot of accidents," Lucas said.

"What?" Eli asked, and then gasped.

A cow had somehow escaped its enclosure and was lumbering onto the road, seemingly out of nowhere. Eli turned the steering wheel expertly and the truck swerved onto the gravel shoulder. Bee smashed into Lucas and Albus yowled and then Lucas yelped as the cat's nails dug into his legs. And the truck skidded to a stop.

It was over almost before it started, and the cow didn't even notice. The truck was humming by the edge of the road, somehow right-side up and untouched. The only damage done was a single box of peaches that had managed to get thrown off the bed, the fruit scattered across the road.

Bee's heart pounded in her chest, and when she swallowed, the sweetness left in her mouth from the peach tasted bitter.

Eli wiped his forehead, breathing deeply through his nose. "Everyone all right?"

"I think so." Lucas took a deep breath, watching the cow lumber across the road and rip up a large strip of grass, roots and all. "And I think I've just solved an important mystery."

Bee turned to him, raising an eyebrow. Had Lucas somehow figured out the million and one questions tumbling around in her head? Like if the green diary didn't originally belong to Eli, who did it belong to? And were they also friends with Alina? And who exactly was that girl in the other memories with the red hair? And most of all, why was the diary now in Alina's cottage? In Bee's experience, you usually only kept things when they meant a great deal to you. She fingered her bracelet, feeling the bumps of the braid under her thumb. The answer to even one of those questions could change everything.

"What? What is it?" Bee breathed.

Lucas smirked. "The mystery of why the cow crossed the road."

· 20 ·

Everyone Loves Gingerbread

Bee walked down the gravel path with her bike, the crunch reminding her of the stale chura snack from earlier, back before her tumble off the bike and the near accident with the cow. Her ankle was much better—she could barely feel it anymore—but now she had other things to worry about. Her heart raced at the thought of what would have happened if the truck hadn't managed to stop in time, or if the cow had been even a little bit slower. Behind them, Eli's truck rumbled off the curb and back onto the highway toward town to replace the sacrificed peaches.

"Come on, Bee, don't be mad." Lucas pet Albus gently, his cheeks flushed for some reason.

Albus was back on his shoulder, fully recovered

from the earlier scare and fast asleep. Bee was beginning to get used to her presence, too; the soft purr in the background was actually relaxing. Although every so often she still felt a second pair of eyes quietly watching.

"It was only a joke—just trying to lighten the mood . . . ," Lucas continued.

Lighten the mood? Did he think pretending everything was going to be okay would make it so? Alina needed their help and they were all out of leads! To make matters worse, the pit in Bee's stomach was back to its rumbling—more than ever now, she needed to see Alina. She needed the magic house where everything was beautiful and safe and perfect, even her own reflection in the mirror.

And where she was friends with someone cool like Alina. Not someone who made jokes about cows. . . .

Bee ground her teeth, trying to hold back all the nasty words that were bubbling up inside her, when Lucas smacked his hand to his forehead. "Why didn't I think of this before?"

Despite her best efforts, Bee let out a snapping retort. "I swear, if you're about to say a knock-knock joke—"

"You wanted to know more about loons!" he exclaimed, speeding up. "And I know someone who knows everything about them, it just didn't occur to me before. Plus, she makes the best cookies, and I don't know about you, but near-death experiences make me peckish. Come on!"

Bee narrowed her eyes suspiciously. "And where does this so-called loon expert live, exactly?"

They'd reached the fork in the road, and Bee peeked nervously at the witch's trailer. A rabbit skirted the unkempt driveway, leaving a trail of pellets in its wake, and a juicy caterpillar inched its way across the fabric of the lawn chair. It was only the second time she'd walked past this place, and already that was two times too many. And then, to Bee's utmost horror, Lucas *turned into the driveway.*

"What are you doing!" Bee gasped, stopping dead in her tracks. "You can't go near there; it's dangerous!"

Lucas glanced back but didn't stop, walking all the way up to the trailer and leaning his bike against the lawn chair. "What's wrong? I thought you wanted loon info." He hurried up the steps and, before Bee could protest, knocked so hard on the door that a few stray pine needles fell from the frail fabric awning above.

The door squeaked open.

"Bee, this is my aunt Gretta," Lucas said. "Auntie, this is my friend Bee."

The bike slipped from Bee's grip as her mouth gaped and her knees went weak. *AUNT?* The Gingerbread Witch was Lucas's aunt?!

"Finally, children! Come inside," a voice called from within.

The scent of gingerbread—earthy nutmeg, spicy ginger, sweet cinnamon—hit Bee full force and she wrestled with the urge to sprint away as fast as possible and the desire to shout out all the questions pressing up behind her lips. Could Alina have been wrong about the witch? Surely anyone related to Lucas wasn't running an evil side gig baking children in their oven. And so it was that Bee felt her feet moving, one small step after another, toward the scariest person she'd ever known. Or so she'd thought.

It took all of one second for Bee to surmise that the gorgeous wood cabin interior, with exposed pine beams and glistening pine walls and a wooden staircase curling up to a second story, was not the inside of the dilapidated trailer she had seen from the outside.

For the second time that summer, Bee was stepping into a magic house, and it wasn't any less impressive. Except there was a theme this time around. Everywhere she looked, there were loons: a collection of acrylic paintings of loons with their chicks hung along the walls, a rug showcasing a loon with its wings outstretched took up most of the floor, small loon carvings and figurines in different poses clustered on the side tables and windowsills and the top of a black wood-burning stove.

The same voice said, "Lucas, you've grown so tall! And Al, so plump and healthy!"

Bee turned to face their host, a tall woman with a squat face, wrapped in a dark red apron. Held in front of her between her oven mitts like a shield was a steaming tray of cookies.

"Hi, Auntie Gretta," Lucas said. "Auntie is the one who gave me Albus a long time ago," he explained.

Bee did a double take. She hadn't recognized her at first, without the usual brown overcoat and hiking boots. Gretta's reddish-brown locks were pulled up into a large bun, showcasing shallow cheeks and sharp, beady eyes. And suddenly, she could see freckles, not unlike Lucas's, dotting her face, and hints of what her hair might have looked like when she was younger: fire-truck red.

"And Bee, nice to see you looking less drowned." Gretta smiled and Bee cringed. "Please, sit. If you're here it must be because you have questions."

The wide L-shaped couch was littered with throw pillows, each one depicting the lake at a different time of day, each printed with the distant silhouette of a loon. Bee moved the pillows over and settled in the deep corner. Lucas sat next to her.

"Help yourselves." Auntie Gretta placed the tray of hot cookies on a wicker place mat in front of them.

Bee reached out politely to take one and froze. The cookies weren't normal cookies. Sure, they were baked to a caramel brown and smelled delicious, but there was something off about them. Each cookie was a picture-perfect miniature replica of a loon. A very, very, *very* realistic replica, detailed down to the textured feathers and sleek pointed beak and webbed feet tucked underneath.

Auntie Gretta chucked (it sounded very close to a cackle, which put Bee further on edge) and grabbed a cookie herself as she sat down.

"Oh, it's all right," she said, biting off the cookie's head. "*These ones* you can eat." She smiled again, showcasing her missing tooth.

Lucas followed her lead, biting into a cookie with gusto. "So good!"

"See, I told you. Everyone loves gingerbread." Gretta placed her hands on her apron and closed her eyes briefly. When she opened them, Bee thought she saw a flash of red. "Now, if you've come to see me, I assume it's because you've discovered Alina is not the kind, gentle child she pretends to be."

"Actually," Lucas piped up, "Bee had some questions about loons—ouch!"

Bee removed her elbow from his side. "Forget about that," she muttered under her breath to Lucas.

They were far beyond loons at this point. Gretta (who may or may not have been a witch) knew about Alina. How? And if she wasn't a witch, why was Alina so afraid of her? Why were these so-called accidents happening? If Alina really did want to hurt Bee, why did she pretend to be Bee's friend? And most of all, what was with all the creepy loon paraphernalia?

Instead, Bee settled with a simple, "Why?"

"Why indeed?" Gretta nodded. "It starts with a new family coming to live in a small town, many years

191

ago, before you or me or even your parents were born."

"The township of Storm," Lucas said.

"Exactly. Unlike many of the other townspeople, who had been living in the same place and working the same farmland for generations, this family came from across the oceans and set up a spice shop on Main Street. They sold herbs and spices the town had never seen before, like turmeric and jeera. I think it's since been converted into a party shop."

Bee's eyes widened—across the oceans, just like her parents. Those were all spices they loved to use in their cooking. Turmeric was essential for a good egg curry, and cumin added a depth of earthy freshness to any good rice biryani. *Alina is like me!*

And then Bee remembered how it felt to be *like her*. What people like Kitty said about people *like her*.

"Did the townspeople treat them . . . differently?" Bee asked.

"Some people were rude. They didn't understand how big the world was." Gretta drummed her fingers on one of her throw pillows. "Alina had a hard time finding where she fit in. The more she tried to make friends, the more the kids pushed her away." She raised her eyebrows at Bee knowingly.

Bee stared at her knees, even though she could feel Lucas's curious gaze burning into her.

"And then things began to happen. It started small—the girls who whispered things behind cupped hands each time Alina was around suddenly became the clumsiest kids in town for an afternoon, tripping over their feet nonstop. Then the neighbor who accidentally forgot to invite Alina to his birthday party had a scare when his brand-new swing set came crashing down the next day. He managed to get off with only a splinter, but it could have been much worse."

Bee's shoulders tensed.

"Slowly, the kids of the township of Storm realized that crossing Alina was dangerous. Which only made them avoid her more. People were growing scared . . . and so were Alina's parents."

"Wait a minute." Lucas scrunched his nose. "I thought they lived on the lake, in that house."

"Indeed. They started off living in town—that's where the shop was, after all. The house on the lake came after . . . the incident."

Incident? Bee wriggled her hands together nervously. *What kind of incident would make them leave?*

"What happened?" she asked.

"The unthinkable." Gretta took a deep breath. "One of the kids went missing."

· 21 ·

Who's Hunting Who

Bee felt frozen in place, her legs and back glued to the sofa. *Alina wouldn't do that, would she?* But she was too afraid to ask. It was like there were two Alinas. There was the girl who went exploring in the dark and wasn't afraid of parents, who took Bee's hand like she was the most important person in the world.

And then there was the girl who seemed to flit in and out of history, making brave kids check over their shoulders and scaring them away from Storm Lake forever.

"He'd been particularly nasty to Alina, poking fun at her behind her back," Gretta said. "It was almost inevitable that she'd get him, too. But don't worry, they found the boy eventually." Bee breathed out in relief.

194

"Alive, albeit a bit worse for wear, wandering the pine forests without a clue how he got there and crumbling little bits of spiced loaf cake as he went."

Bee instinctively brought her arms around herself, as though chasing away a chill. "What did Alina's parents do?" she asked.

"The only thing they could do. Leave. One day, the spice shop was up and running, walls full to bursting with bins of ingredients. The next day, it was all gone," Gretta continued. "It was as if they'd never moved in."

"Why?" Lucas asked, petting Albus. "Where did the family go?"

"Not the whole family. Just the parents. Sadly, they abandoned Alina," Gretta said. "Not long after, a house appeared just outside town. A big house with a nice garden and a rose-covered trellis."

"The house across the lake," Bee said.

Gretta nodded. "It was the first cottage on the lake, but it wasn't a normal one. Some say the parents had it built special, to stop Alina from getting out. Some say Alina built the house herself with all the things a little girl could ever dream of inside, which is why she never left. . . . Townsfolk went to check up on things, of course, curious as to what happened to the girl."

"And?" Lucas croaked.

"Don't know. No one ever came back."

Bee swallowed hard, remembering how safe it had felt inside the magic house at night, how beautiful and wonderful it had all seemed, made just for her.

"I don't get it." Lucas shook his head.

Auntie Gretta shrugged. "That's the mystery, isn't it. It's an abandoned lot. Except on some nights, when the moon is high and the lake is dark, the lights come on inside. Alina is still there, unable to wander too far from the property. And she'll do anything—show you things you didn't think possible, make you feel like you are the most important person in the world to her—to change that."

Lucas made a noise that sounded like he'd just swallowed his tongue. He sat up straight, pointing at his goggles in disbelief, then smacking a fist on the coffee table. "I knew ghosts were real!"

But Bee wasn't listening. *This is my favorite place to explore, right here.* That's what Alina had told her on that sunny day, the first time they met. The truth was much more sinister. Alina *couldn't* leave. Except . . . Bee frowned.

"But she visited me, the day it rained," Bee muttered.

There was a shift in Gretta's posture. Her long arms turned stiff as branches, and her eyes grew harder than stone, and Bee could have sworn a few of the red loon eyes around the room swiveled her way.

"Then you've found some bread crumbs," she said slowly.

Lucas raised an eyebrow.

"Memories tied to objects," Gretta explained. "All ghosts have them. They're created by the people who cared for them once upon a time. And as long as the bread crumbs exist, ghosts are able to walk among us. The bad ones like Alina, but the good ones, too."

The braided bracelet suddenly felt heavy on Bee's wrist, and she rubbed her hands together.

"Alina *is* a good one." Bee's jaw tensed. Surely not everything Alina said was a lie. "She's really scared and asked *me* to help her. Alina believes someone is hunting her."

"My dear." Gretta sighed, and it sounded like the wind sliding between pine branches. "She may seem like a 'good one,' but with Alina, nothing is as it seems. Make no mistake, *she* is the one hunting *you*."

A chill crept around Bee's ankles, running up her legs and settling with a nauseating pulse in the pit of her stomach. She reached up and twisted a loose strand of hair around her finger. *I like your hair*, Alina had said, her eyes large and her lips curved. Doubt blossomed like a rotten flower. The bold words, the mischievous grins, the arm around Bee's shoulders.

But there was a part of Bee that didn't believe that Alina was dangerous. She couldn't be. Maybe if those township kids hadn't been so mean, she wouldn't have hurt that boy. Maybe if someone had given her a chance to be herself, things wouldn't have escalated and the house across the lake wouldn't have been built. Maybe if Alina could see what she'd become, could see how she'd changed, she would realize there was another way.

It wasn't possible Alina was lying about everything, was it? *I'm sure she really is my friend.*

"How do you know all this?" Bee asked.

Gretta leaned forward. "Who do you think was the first kid Alina tried to trap? Why do you think I've stayed here all these years since? Hm?"

Bee hiccuped as the images from the candle and the bike rushed back. Images of a strong girl with long ginger hair who wasn't scared to fight back. *No. Way.*

Gretta's eyes glistened. "I stayed to make sure it doesn't happen again. I tried to warn you, by the way, with those dreams. . . . And the loons have been doing their best to peck holes in all the boats around this lake so you couldn't get back to *her.* We try to stop all the kids who get lured toward the abandoned house. But you just couldn't keep away, could you."

The loons? "We"? Bee was suddenly acutely aware of all the loons in the room, from the pillows to the paintings to the figurines. And it felt as if they were all watching her. She inched closer to Lucas, who appeared to be completely oblivious to what was going on. She had always suspected the loons weren't normal birds. But after meeting Gretta (who definitely wasn't baking anything other than gingerbread in her oven, as far as Bee could tell), she had thought maybe, just maybe, the whole loon thing was in her imagination.

Bee exhaled shakily. "So . . . you're *not* a witch?"

Of course she's not a witch, Bee thought the second the words left her lips. Her cheeks reddened. *Alina only said that because she was scared you'd learn the truth and leave her!*

But Gretta didn't even flinch at the accusation. After a minute, a smile crept across her thin lips. "I never said that."

She winked, and Bee's hurt drummed.

"What do we do now?" Lucas asked, reaching for another cookie. "Alina is after Bee. She's been getting into accidents. And Eli said the only way to stop it is to run away."

"The bread crumbs are the key," Gretta said, standing. "We need to gather all the bread crumbs together, make sure there aren't any more, and destroy them. It's the only way to stop Alina and trap her in that house. Forever."

Bee's heart drummed faster. *Destroy?* This didn't feel right. It didn't feel right at all. A drop of moisture slid down her frizzy hair and across her brow as Gretta—no, the Gingerbread Witch—fixed her with those hard eyes.

"Tell me, Bee, have you found all the bread crumbs? Because if there is even one left, that ghost will continue to haunt you."

Bee swallowed hard, feeling a tenseness creep into her shoulders like hard, bony fingers.

"Because *if* there is another bread crumb," Gretta continued, "the more you wish you weren't so different, the more you wish you could fit in, the more Alina's power will continue to grow."

The bony fingers moved to her stomach as Gretta continued, tying it into knots. It was a horrible sensation, the kind that keeps you up at night, sweating under the blankets but too scared to come up for air.

"And the more you keep thinking about Alina, the more time you spend in that house of hers at night, the more you'll want to go back—like an insatiable hunger."

Gretta leaned forward, her mouth set with worry. "I have a feeling that if you ever go back inside that house—Bee, you might never be able to leave."

Bee steadied her breathing, not daring to glance at Lucas. "No, I think we found all of them. There aren't any more."

"Good," Gretta said, taking the tray of cookies and offering another to Bee, all without breaking her gaze. "This will all be over soon, then."

Bee didn't look away, either, taking a cookie even though she wasn't hungry. Even though she wanted time to clear her head and figure things out, as far away as possible from Gretta and the trailer and the loons. But she knew if she did, if she moved her gaze even an inch, Gretta would know she was lying.

• 22 •

Bad Things Happen in Threes

Rain clouds were moving in across the blue sky, and the hammering of a woodpecker resonated through the forest. If her dad were there, he would have insisted they stop and scour the trees, craning their necks for a glimpse of the bird's red cap above. Woodpeckers were rare in the city, and her dad always hung suet cakes around the house in winter to coax them out. There wouldn't be any stopping for bird spotting today, though.

Bee walked briskly up the Gladers' driveway, her pockets light, her hands empty, and her feet kicking up dead leaves and pine needles. At Gretta's urging, they had left the other bread crumbs behind at the trailer. And although Bee had pretended to be okay about it at the time, she didn't have to pretend now that she was alone. Her hands formed into fists at the words that had been circling her mind nonstop, like a water spider stuck in the whirlpool of a canoe paddle.

I need to go back.

Alina might have been strange, maybe even dangerous. But no one stuck up for her back then, no one ever gave her a proper chance. And now, without any bread crumbs, Alina would be stuck in that house alone forever! *I need to go back and help her.* But it wasn't so simple.

Gretta's words echoed in Bee's head like a loon's cry—high-pitched and eerie. *You might never be able to leave.* Plus, trapping Alina in the house would only make her loneliness worse . . . and make her more dangerous. Why did everything have to be so complicated?

All Bee knew for sure was that running away and forgetting all about Alina wasn't going to fix things. The only real solution was to confront her head-on with the truth—the final bread crumb, waiting patiently in the magic library: the diary.

The chill that had caught hold of her earlier made its way into her bones, and it felt like being plunged into icy water. *You don't have to be scared. You know Alina. You'll just talk, and everything will be explained,* Bee reasoned. But something told her there was more to the story.

Bee had just put a hand on the canoe when a voice

made her stop in her tracks.

"Binita Bakshi, where do you think you're going?"

Her mom stood on the porch in a brilliant orange sarong, arms crossed and hair loose. Bee would have described her as beautiful in the moment, if it hadn't been for the scowl on her face and the smoke coming out of her ears (all right, there wasn't any smoke, but by the look on her face there might as well have been). Through the living room window, Bee could see her father watching from inside the cottage.

Uh-oh. This couldn't have happened at a worse time. Bee didn't have time for angry parents right now! Reluctantly, she walked back toward the cottage, stopping at the bottom of the deck steps. Up close, her mom was even more scary looking, with flames dancing in her eyes and her hair curling around her head like a crown. She'd never seen her mom so upset.

Bee took a deep breath. "Whatever it is I did, I'm really sorry and I'll make up for it later, but right now I need to take the canoe out. Please!"

"You'll make up for it?" her mom said, her words like daggers. "You won't believe who I ran into this morning. The Lafleurs; our neighbors."

Oh no. Bee was starting to have a very good idea what this was about.

"Very pleasant. They live three houses down from us," her mom continued. "And I was chatting about the weather, and how it was supposed to be nice out tomorrow, thank goodness. You know, for Granny's party. It didn't take me long to realize that they never got an invitation. No one did."

Bee's cheeks burned. "I didn't mean to—"

"Ah." Mrs. Bakshi held up a finger to indicate she wasn't finished, and Bee promptly clammed up. "And guess what else went missing today? Another six jars of my peach pickle! There's barely any left!"

Bee frowned. She'd only taken one. "But that wasn't me!"

"No, that's enough," Mrs. Bakshi snapped. "I know it was you. Your father found a pickle jar on the dock the other day, and don't think I haven't noticed you taking the canoe out all the time. We didn't teach you to hurt others like this. Because this is very hurtful, to your dad and me, and to Granny. And you're going to make up for it right now. Tell me again how you have something more important to do than going out and inviting our wonderful neighbors to your dear grandmother's party?"

Bee grimaced at the impossibility of the situation. Because she *did* have something more important to do— namely, stop Alina from luring kids into her haunted house for all eternity. Before a certain witch took matters into her own hands. The problem was, there was no way her mom would believe her.

"I still have to go," Bee said quietly.

Her mom's shoulders slumped suddenly, the fire

in her eyes winking out. "I don't understand, Binita. You've been acting strange all week, trying to get out of helping with this party. Why didn't you deliver the invitations the first time? And why did you take my jars of peach pickle?"

Bee hung her head. Her parents were always so confident, acting like they didn't care what other people thought. . . . How could she make them understand that she didn't mean to hurt anybody? Tears pushed at the backs of her eyes.

Bee muttered quickly, keeping her voice low so that it sounded like one long word. "I didn't deliver the invitations because I didn't want everyone coming over and seeing how weird our family is and I really didn't want you handing out pickles to everyone—no one does that around here."

"What?" Her mom's voice cracked. "What do you mean, *weird*?"

The nape of Bee's neck flushed hot as she lifted her chin and took a breath. And said the words she always bit back—the words she was too afraid to say out loud.

"We're different, Mom. Can't you see how people look at us? It's just embarrassing!" Bee said. "You think Betsy Chillers is too scary, when literally every kid in school is reading it. You just don't get it. We're nothing like Kitty's family, and you and Dad don't even try to fit in. Inviting the neighbors over would be like telling people to come look at how weird we are, and people already think I'm different enough. I don't want to end up a total weirdo like Lucas, okay? With no friends except for an old cat that he carries everywhere."

Bee looked up, hoping her mom would understand, but her mom's eyes shifted toward the wood shelter. Bee followed her gaze. *Lucas.* He stood there with his mouth slightly ajar and eyebrows puckered, Albus curled around his neck.

Her chest squeezed. *Maybe he didn't hear?*

"Lucas." Bee stepped toward him, but his expression crumpled and he shot back into the forest. "Mom?" She turned back slowly, but her mom only shook her head.

The clouds continued to race by, casting shadows one second and letting the sunshine through the next.

"Sweetheart, Lucas carries that cat around everywhere because it helps him cope. The cat was a gift he got the day his dad passed away. I thought you were friends. Didn't he tell you?"

His dad? Bee's head was pounding, her chest tight. A sudden wave of nausea was threatening to crash down.

"Go after him. The invitations can wait," her mom said. "Hurt that is left to fester will only grow into something worse. You have to fix things and show him who you really are."

Something worse. Bee glanced toward the lake, where the pines camouflaged the abandoned lot and where, in a few hours, she'd have to confront that something. She glanced at her mom, who, despite everything Bee had done, was wrapping her in loving words and forgiveness just like she'd wrapped the towels around her that morning and lifted her from the lake. And then Bee took off, racing into the woods, picking her way along the shortcut trail between the two properties.

Lucas was nothing like Kitty. He wasn't cool, his parents didn't take him to fancy amusement parks, and he didn't have lots of friends. But Lucas was *always* ready to help and had instantly believed her when she told him about the witch. Plus, he never made fun of her parents' food or the fact that her hair was a tad on the frizzy side. *I don't deserve such a good friend.* And now he was the only person who could help her.

Bee ignored the leaves slapping her in the face and burst out next to Lucas's cottage just in time to see him speed out of the driveway on his bike.

"Lucas, wait!" she yelled, racing after him through the cloud of dust he left behind. "Come back!"

The trees rustled and black-capped chickadees chirped merrily, and Lucas didn't slow down. *I didn't mean to say those things, I didn't know you were standing there!* Bee breathed in heavily, slowing down as the bike sped up the hill and disappeared around the corner. Bits of gravel had snuck into her sandals, poking the soles of her feet.

Bee crouched by the side of the road, burying her head in her arms. She had hurt Lucas when all he'd done was help her. She'd hurt her parents when all they wanted was to plan a celebration together. And as for Granny . . .

Her chest heaved as tears prickled in the corners of her eyes. *I messed up everything.* Granny would have known what to say, even if that meant not saying anything as she shuffled back and forth between the stove and the table, bringing another chapati with her each time for Bee to butter with ghee. That was her—how did Lucas put it?—her favorite time.

"I wouldn't say you messed up *everything*," a familiar voice sang in Bee's ear.

She looked up at the crinkled brown face beaming in the shadow of an oversize pink sun hat, and felt a few new tears push their way to the corners of her eyes.

"Granny! You're here!"

"Of course I am, bright-eyed and bushy-tailed!" Granny exclaimed, placing a hand on Bee's shoulder to steady herself, the way she did on their walks. "Where else would I be when my granddaughter needs me? My beautiful granddaughter, with so much light in her heart."

Bee blushed and cleaned the tear stains from her glasses on the hem of her shirt. Then she slowly stood up, a part of her still floating in the memory of hot ghee and burned flour. "It's just . . . you've been disappearing lately. And things have been . . . so complicated. I don't know what to do."

Granny pursed her lips in thought, and as she did, she began to hum softly.

"Granny?" Bee asked, waiting. She recognized the humming as "Memory" from the musical *Cats*. But Granny didn't seem to hear her. She turned and began to wander away down the gravel path. "Wait, don't you need help walking back to the cottage?"

Granny briefly interrupted her humming to put a hand up and wave Bee away. "Don't worry about me, I'll be here when you need me."

Bee closed her eyes as the humming was replaced with the sounds of the forest again. She listened to the whisper of the wind in the leaves, and the whine of mosquitoes, and the crunch of a bike over gravel. *Wait a second!*

Bee lifted her head as the bike squealed to a stop.

"Why are you just standing there?" Lucas asked. Albus meowed sleepily from his shoulders, tilting her head to one side and pushing it into his neck affectionately. "It's getting kinda dark."

The hurt she'd seen earlier was gone, and his cheeks were back to their gloriously annoying cheerfulness.

"Lucas!" Bee practically jumped toward him. "I'm so sorry about earlier. And I'm sorry about Albus. I've been a terrible friend, and I don't think you're a weirdo."

Lucas turned a deep shade of purple. "Oh yeah, I figured. You were upset, and sometimes things come out wrong when you're upset. My mom says that, anyways."

"Then why did you race away?"

"Oh." Lucas brought a hand to his hair. "I didn't figure that out right away. I guess at first I was upset, too, about what you said." He glanced away. "But I'm glad I heard, because now I know that you're a bit like me."

"What?" Bee asked.

"You know . . . school problems. Some kids can be really mean, but it's not everyone."

Bee felt her cheeks warm, too. From the beginning, she hadn't been fair. But she wanted to be friends this time. Real friends. And real friends knew things like why there was a cat living on someone's shoulder. "Can I ask you something?"

Lucas unbuckled his helmet. "Sure."

"Why do you wear those goggles? I mean, what's the real reason?" *And why would you choose to be different?*

Lucas hung the helmet on his handlebar next to a brown paper bag. "I've never had many friends, but I've always liked spooky stuff, especially ghosts. My dad was really into ghosts, too, and we made up this game where we'd put goggles on and go ghost hunting. I knew it was all pretend, but it was still fun." His voice softened, and Bee had to strain to catch his words. "When he left, I started wearing the goggles to school because somehow it felt like he was still there. And that maybe this way, if he really was a ghost, I'd be able to see him again."

Tears prickled Bee's eyes again. She'd lost someone recently, too, someone who understood the hard bits that came with having parents like hers and a friend like Kitty, someone special, whose mere presence made everything okay again. Someone Bee wasn't ready to talk about. She brushed the bracelet with her thumb.

"I'm sorry about your dad."

"It's all right." Lucas took a deep breath. "If I was different before, I was a straight-up weirdo at school after that. That's when Mom decided to try home-schooling. She says in a year or so we'll try again at a new school. What about you? Do you have friends?"

Bee frowned. "I have friends," she said quickly, but for the first time, she wasn't so sure. "But I still don't fit in, no matter how hard I try. Anyways, I'm sorry I called you a weirdo."

Lucas adjusted his goggles. "I'm not. I'd rather be a weirdo and not belong than change myself just to fit in."

Bee started to talk, then stopped. She'd been trying so hard to fit in at school and with Kitty that she never once considered that she was changing who she really was. The bejeweled cell phone case that looked like the other girls', even though, if she really thought about it, sparkles weren't her thing; turning her nose up at her mom's peach pickle even though it was delicious . . . *Is that really me?*

"Anyways," she stuttered, "are we cool?"

"Yeah, we're cool." The wind blew stronger and dark clouds raced across the sky. "So do you really think going back to Alina is a good idea?"

Bee's heart skipped a beat. Had it been that obvious that she was lying earlier? And worse, what if Gretta had picked up on it, too? *You might never be able to leave.* That's what Gretta had said. But for Bee, the risk was worth it. She smoothed back her frizzy hair, preparing another half-truth.

"I'm only going back because I forgot something there," Bee started. "I, er, think I left my shoes there the other day. . . ."

Lucas raised a red eyebrow, and even Albus the cat seemed to tilt her head skeptically. Bee bit her lip. *Note to self: think of a better excuse next time!*

Thankfully, Lucas cut her off. "Eli talked about a green diary when he gave us a ride. It's the last bread crumb, isn't it?"

Bee was reminded once again how much Lucas paid attention, and waited for the lecture about how it wasn't safe and Alina was too dangerous and blah, blah, blah. But it never came.

"Aren't you going to tell me not to go?" Bee asked.

Lucas shrugged. "Actually, I was kind of hoping you would ask me to help. You *were* about to ask, weren't you?"

Bee blinked a few times, surprised. Now that she thought about it, of course it would be better if Lucas came, especially if Alina was as dangerous as everyone seemed to believe. Bee knew how he felt about Alina, and it had never seemed fair to ask him to come—but it had never occurred to her that he would *want* to come.

Albus stirred on his shoulder and let out a gigantic yawn, and Lucas put a hand on Bee's arm. "You don't have to answer." His cheeks reddened. "I'll help you no matter what."

Bee's heart beat a little faster as her eyes met his, and he jumped back, embarrassed. "So what's the plan? What are we going to do?"

So it was settled. Lucas was coming with her. Bee breathed out a slow sigh of relief. There was still one tiny problem, though.

"My parents are still going to be mad at me," she said. "There's no way they're going to let me canoe across the lake. And I still have to do something about tomorrow's party. . . . What are you smiling about?"

A grin was spreading across his face. "While you were feeling sorry for yourself, I went and grabbed something." He reached into the brown paper bag on his handlebars, revealing a plate full of cookies. Loon-shaped gingerbread cookies. "For when you invite the neighbors. Everyone likes gingerbread."

Bee peered at him suspiciously, noting the new crumbs decorating the front of his polo. Was Lucas always this nice, and she had just never noticed? She took the plate with a small smile. "That's . . . really nice of you, actually. Thanks."

Lucas stuck his helmet back on, flattening his flaming-red hair. "No problem. So about tonight, do you think you could sneak out after your parents go to sleep?"

"You mean after dark?" It was Bee's turn to grin. *I can definitely do that.*

· 23 ·

You're Not Welcome Here

The moon was full when Bee slipped out her bedroom window and stole down the dewy grass toward the dock. The lake winked with the reflection of the sky, filled with a million billion miniature suns. But there was cold wind blowing with an urgency that made Bee anxious. She quelled the squigglies brewing in her belly, wondering whether Alina would even show herself tonight, or if she would hide like she did during the day when Bee had called for her from the rubble of the house. *And what if she does come, what then?*

Alina was a formidably powerful and daring girl, and Bee could only imagine how powerful she would become if Bee got on her bad side. She tried to comfort herself with the fact that she wouldn't be alone.

For once, Albus was on the ground sniffing at the edge of the cattails while Lucas stood by the water looking across the lake, removing his sandals and shirt before pulling on a life jacket.

"Hey, what are you doing?" Bee asked, slightly alarmed. With just his swim trunks and the ever-present goggles, it almost looked like Lucas had no intention of using the canoe. . . .

Bee tried to locate the canoe in the small swamp, but it wasn't there. Instead, the three loons appeared to be waiting nearby, while keeping their distance from a curious Albus.

"Where's the canoe?" Bee asked, panic in her voice. Without the canoe, they couldn't possibly get across the lake!

Lucas played with the fasteners of his life jacket before putting it on the ground. "Auntie Gretta warned me this might happen," he said, walking to the edge of the dock and testing the water with his big toe. "She said Alina might take the canoe."

Bee grimaced. At first it was the loons trying to stop her from crossing the lake, and now it was Alina herself! She didn't like the direction this was taking. Not one bit.

"Then why don't we use your canoe, or another neighbor's boat?" she asked. "I'm sure someone has a small rowboat we can borrow."

Even as she said the words, Bee knew that Alina

would have taken care of that. There wouldn't be another canoe or rowboat or paddleboard anywhere near the lake tonight. Clearly, Bee had upset the ghost, and Alina was making it pretty obvious she didn't want any visitors.

Bee groaned as she realized Lucas's intention. *Of course.* "I am *not* swimming."

Lucas turned back, throwing a pair of goggles her way. "Your mom mentioned you're a strong swimmer, though, aren't you?"

"I can't do it, Lucas, I'm serious." Bee picked up her life jacket, discarded near the water, then walked to the end of the dock and sat down. Her knees felt weak and her mouth was dry. It wasn't something she'd admitted to anyone, not even Kitty. "Lake water . . . scares me."

Bee startled as Lucas took a seat beside her. She hadn't heard him walk up.

"There's no other way, though," he said softly. "If it makes you feel better, I'm a terrible swimmer, and I'll go with you."

"Meow!" Albus agreed.

Bee frowned. "Albus?" She peered into the dark, but the cat was nowhere to be seen.

"Meow!"

Lucas and Bee shared an equally puzzled look, before peering over the edge of the dock. And they gulped as Albus came into view, an orange ball of fluff *perched on the back of a loon*, who seemed much too calm about the whole situation. The loon watched Bee with its red eyes for a second and then headed out deeper into the water, bringing Albus along with it.

"Marvelous!" gasped Lucas.

Slowly, he lowered himself into the water as a second loon swam around the corner.

"What are you doing?" hissed Bee. Sure, the loons worked with Gretta, but that didn't mean they weren't still wild!

But the loon didn't seem wild at all. It waited by Lucas patiently until he placed his hands on its back like a flutterboard. Immediately the loon started forward, slicing through the water like a knife through soft ghee. Bee recalled the feeling of something sleek and strong carrying her forward after the canoe tipped, and how realistic Gretta's gingerbread loon cookies were. A waft of gingerbread came from the lake as the third and final loon swam forward, waiting for her.

"You're here to help us?" Bee asked. The loon of course did not respond (animals don't talk, obviously), but cocked its head knowingly.

Clouds were slowly gathering to block out the stars. Bee peered across the lake, watching the small shapes of Lucas and Albus. If the loons held a grudge toward her for using the peach pickle on them, they didn't show it. Cautiously, she removed her sweater, leaving on her T-shirt and shorts, and zipped up the life jacket.

Maybe Lucas felt comfortable without it, but she didn't. Bee stepped onto the ladder. The water was cold as it swirled around her ankles and legs. She snapped the goggles over her eyes, shading the dark lake purple with the lens.

You can do this. Be fearless, like Betsy Chillers.

Bee braced herself and pushed off the ladder toward the loon. Her breath came in quick puffs as the cold seeped into her skin. *Calm down, you have to calm down.* With a gargantuan effort, Bee kicked her legs, shaking out the tense muscles. Carefully, she placed her hands on the loon's back. It was as though she'd flicked the switch on a motorboat, except there was no sound, no roar, no bubbles. They simply shot forward into the dark, the water peeling away from Bee as her body floated up behind from the momentum.

This time, Bee didn't close her eyes. The upper layer of water was warmer, and the stars winked in the lake as she passed through. They were moving much faster than she could have swum or even paddled in the canoe. In no time at all, they reached the other side, where the stolen canoe lay waiting.

"That was wild," she breathed to Lucas, whose wet hair was already springing back into ringlets at odd angles. "I can't believe I did that."

Lucas gave Bee a helping hand up onto shore. Albus was back on his shoulders. The loons, however, stayed firmly in the water, ruffling their feathers uncomfortably.

The air was heavy with a cold humidity, and a familiar spicy scent wafted up.

Bee's toe caught in a glob of something oily and cold as she huddled in her life jacket for warmth.

"Yuck." Bee lifted her foot. "Peach pickle." *So that's where the missing jars went.*

It was splattered around the lake's edge like some kind of barrier. Alina definitely didn't want any visitors tonight.

Lucas wrung water from the hem of his swim trunks as they faced the cobblestone path. "So this is what it looks like at night, huh? Way creepier."

Bee wriggled the pickle off her foot and quickly swept the patio and stone wall with her eyes. Lucas was right. There was no rose-covered archway or waiting tea set this time. The warm, magical welcome she'd received last time was gone.

"Alina doesn't want us here," Bee whispered, goose bumps running up her wet legs. The pine needles were prickly under her bare feet. "Are you sure you want to come?"

"Oh no, you're not doing this again." Lucas scowled. "I'm not letting you go alone."

He pushed his hair out of his face and marched forward, and Bee had no choice but to follow. And the more they walked, the more Bee realized how right her first impression had been. Everything about the property had been slightly altered to make it as unwelcoming as possible. The cobblestone pathway was three times as long, winding through a grove of pines and over a field of dry, uncomfortable pinecones before reaching the sandstone wall. But it wasn't the same wall; this time, there was no rickety archway and no steps leading through it. The only way forward was to climb.

Lucas made it look easy, scrambling up over the wall first. Clearly all the practice rolling and dodging ghosts at the market had paid off. Bee, on the other hand, was more of the do-anything-to-get-out-of-gym-class type. Gingerly, she gripped the sharp edges of the stones, hoisting herself upward using the tips of her fingers and toes to find hidden hand- and footholds. Her feet were wet and cold from the water, and pine needles stuck out between her toes.

"Nearly there," Lucas said encouragingly, and Bee grimaced.

Hands trembling, hair soaked (there was that drowned-rat aesthetic again), and limbs splayed across the embarrassingly low wall, this wasn't her best moment. But Bee brought first one hand up, then one foot, and slowly made it over.

Ahead, the gentle slope of grass drew their gaze toward the hulking outline of the intact house. Whereas before everything about the house had been like a hand ushering Bee inside, now it stood menacing and grim, like a fortress. It loomed against the dark, cloudy sky, brown wood paneling and gingerbread trim relegated to the shadows, cracks spidering across the windows, the trellises of roses replaced with weeds and thorny thistles.

"You're telling me that during the daytime, this mansion is a heap of rubble?" Lucas asked as they reached the entrance. Some kind of white fungus crept around the edges of the door handle.

"Yup." Bee nodded, noting the overgrown grass and dried-up vines climbing the stone facade and front balcony. There wasn't a single light on. "You still want to go in with me?"

Lucas chuckled uneasily and Bee quelled the nerves building up inside her. *This is it. It's time to talk to a ghost.*

She pushed the door open as big juicy raindrops began to splotch the house, and they stepped inside.

· 24 ·

The Shadow in the Mirror

"It's all different from before," Bee said. "Definitely not the same."

The watercolor paintings and pretty burgundy walls were gone, replaced with chipped paint and creeping moss. Orange-and-pink flames burst to life in the living room fireplace, as though detecting their presence. The picture frame on the mantel was no longer there. Bee turned to survey the furniture, now cracked and splintered, the stuffing from the plump chairs and couches gouged out.

"Definitely creepy," whined Lucas, keeping close. For once, Albus was wide awake, her green eyes glowing in the dim light.

The state of the house didn't matter. What mattered

was finding Alina and finding out the truth. Which meant that Bee needed to get her hands on that green diary. The chime of children's laughter ran along the empty hallway. Bee turned to face the direction of the sound, but Lucas didn't react—as if the laughter was only meant for Bee's ears.

"So we're looking for a library, right?" Lucas asked. "It's probably going to be somewhere on the main floor, this way. That's where my mom keeps her books."

Bee stepped away from the crackling fireplace— there was no warmth coming off the fire this time, as though it was just an illusion.

"I'm not sure," she said, peering back toward the kitchen. "I think I remember the library being upstairs. Either way, I don't think we should split up . . . Lucas?"

Suddenly, Bee was distinctly aware of how quiet he was. When she turned, Lucas was gone. Bee clenched her fists, unsure whether to be terrified or frustrated. *Betsy Chillers's third rule of thumb: Don't separate!* She exhaled. This wasn't the time to think about how annoying Lucas was.

Footsteps resonated from up the stairs. Was Alina already up there, waiting for her? The house moaned as a strong gust of wind swept across the lake, rattling the windows and shaking the door. Bee glanced back nervously at the front door before deciding to follow the footsteps.

It didn't take long for Bee to find the light switch.

The flickering lightbulb flooded the steps in a cold light and the wood creaked ominously as she climbed, as though unsure if it wanted to break under her weight or not. Her heart thudded and her breath sounded loud. Too loud.

"I know you're up here, Alina!" she called.

Bee could picture her now, with her large eyes and dark curls and perfect pout, grinning mischievously at her plans to spook Bee and Lucas. Little did Alina know, after a lifetime of reading Betsy Chillers, Bee knew a thing or two about ghosts. It would only take a minute to get the diary from the bookshelf and find out the truth, and then she could talk to Alina. Easy.

But something halted Bee in her tracks.

The library door was open, but there were no trees or books. And no Alina. Bee gritted her teeth—was this the wrong room? *I could have sworn the library was around here somewhere. . . .*

Instead, white curtains billowed in front of the open balcony doors of an old bedroom with black-and-white-striped wallpaper. A large bed was piled high with cushions, the sheets so full of holes from hungry moth larvae that they looked more like lace. A dusty vanity sat next to the bed, and directly behind it . . . *a bookshelf!*

Bee walked across the mossy carpet toward it. The carpet smelled like old shoes, and baby moths fluttered up around her legs as she moved. Somehow, the bookshelf seemed to be the only section of the room that hadn't succumbed to decay. Maybe, just maybe, the diary would be there. Could she be that lucky? Bee ran a finger along the familiar spines of Betsy Chillers books. Her shoulders slumped—no, it wasn't there. Had she misremembered where the library was after all?

The sound of creaking footsteps floated up from the stairs.

She sighed, turning toward the bedroom door. "You were right, Lucas. The library must be—"

The words faded from Bee's mouth. The door was still wide open and the footsteps had stopped, but there was no one there. Another gust of wind pushed through the open balcony, billowing the curtains out, and the night air made Bee shiver in her still damp clothes. A handful of raindrops splattered onto the carpet.

Bee swallowed hard, goose bumps climbing the back of her neck.

"Alina?" she called out tentatively. "Is that you? I just want to talk."

The gossamer curtain swelled with wind again, and Bee's pulse quickened. *She's one of the good ones*, Bee repeated to herself silently, like a mantra. *She just needs a chance.* She let out a breath slowly, trying not to think of the stories Gretta had told them. The stories about all those kids.

"I know you've been hurting people, Alina," she

said, "and I know you don't mean to." Bee scoured the room as she talked, peering into the shadows for any sign of a flicker, any sign that Alina was listening. "You're lonely, and that's okay. I get lonely, too, sometimes. But there's another way to make friends, and I'll prove it to you. I just need you to show me where the library is first."

Bee turned, catching a glimpse of her own reflection in the vanity mirror. But there was no frizz-free hair or perfect complexion or blue romper this time. It was just Bee, with her thick-rimmed glasses and wet life jacket—just the truth. Her chest tightened. Behind her reflection was an empty bookshelf, covered in an inch of dust and cobwebs. *What?*

Bee frowned, checking over her shoulder. Sure enough, the glossy spines of Betsy Chillers novels stared back at her. And yet the mirror showed a bookshelf that looked to have been empty for over a century. Bee squinted into the mirror. Not completely empty. There was something there, hidden under the dust. Something with a spiral spine.

Bee backed up slowly, keeping an eye on the mirror and reaching back toward the shelf. And then she froze. There was a shadow in the mirror now, a shadow that hadn't been there before, standing between her and the bookshelf, only a few steps away.

"Lies," a voice whispered. "I saw you."

The shadow flickered like a flame and Bee's pulse

quickened. *Is that . . . Alina?*

"Saw me where?" Bee asked. *She's one of the good ones. She just needs a chance.*

"I saw you with that witch. And that boy," Alina answered. "Hatching plans against me, just like they did back then."

"They"? Bee swallowed hard, ignoring the subtle wobble in the floor planks. Trying to keep her hand from shaking. This was obviously a misunderstanding. Anyway, how would Alina know they had talked to Gretta? Then she remembered the bread crumbs they had left at Gretta's trailer—the torn pages about the loons, the candle stub, and the bike with its bell. *Wherever the bread crumbs go, Alina can go, too.* Alina had heard everything. And she was angry.

Bee's heart thudded against her rib cage. Cautiously, slowly, without taking her eyes off the mirror, she slid a foot backward again, trying to maneuver around the shadow that could only be Alina. Instantly, the carpet below her quivered. As if it wasn't simply a carpet, as if the wooden floorboards underneath weren't simply planks of wood, but something . . . living.

She doesn't believe me. She doesn't believe that I'm not going to hurt her.

Bee took a breath, willing her voice to sound earnest, and willing Alina to believe her. "I would never hurt you. We only went to see Gret—I mean, the witch—for answers. Please trust me; I'm only here to help you!"

The floor wobbled again, letting out an ominous creak, like the warning of a lightning bolt snapping through the air.

"Liar!" The whisper was no longer a whisper but a hollow wail, filling up the space with the scent of marsh water. "I can feel him lurking about, poking at my walls, touching things he shouldn't. You're not alone here. And I know what you're looking for."

And then the shadow in the mirror shifted, and for a second Bee thought she saw something. Something without a hint of the delicate features and mischievous grin Bee had come to know. Something that could never have had eyes that sparkled with adventure. Something that made Bee doubt that the ghost that was Alina had any good left in her.

A sound like heavy rain started up. Alina was inhaling. Then in a final thundering scream that shook the walls and brought Bee to her knees, the ghost spoke her last words: "You're not welcome here!"

And then the room collapsed.

• 25 •

A Trap Is Set

Bee yelped as the floor wobbled again. All around her, the walls shuddered and the curtains were ripped from their rods and the door seemed to be swallowing itself whole—the doorframe collapsing and the only way out quickly disappearing.

"Wait, Alina!" she called out as the shadow streaked across the bookshelf. "I just want to help!"

The shadow flickered, as though considering the offer, before slowly sinking down the shelves and disappearing into the floor. Bee gritted her teeth, trying to keep the gnawing hunger in her belly at bay. Alina was gone, along with the notebook. What was going to happen now? Was Gretta right? Was the best thing for everyone to destroy all the bread crumbs? Bee's chest tightened.

There was no time to dwell. She brought her hands up to shield her face. Bee was in the eye of a storm, a terrible, angry storm of wood splintering and carpets undulating likes waves on the lake when the wind grew too strong.

Wait a second. . . . Bee peered through her fingers as a falling chunk of ceiling very obviously swerved around her at the last second, avoiding her. Slowly Bee lowered her hands, observing the clouds of dust and floating debris. And noting how so far, nothing seemed to actually fall *on* her. She was completely unharmed.

And then she saw it. Caught one last glimpse of the vanity mirror before a crack spiderwebbed across its surface. The diary. The diary was still on the bookshelf. Hope licked tentatively around Bee's thoughts, like the flowery vines that had grown along the outside of Alina's house that one magical night—*I can still do this! I can still help Alina!* Bee swiveled around and lurched toward the bookshelf, leaping over the carpet that tried to wrap itself around her feet. There were no other books anymore, no glossy Betsy Chillers spines. Only layers of dust and the diary.

And then, just as quickly, Bee realized her mistake. The balcony was gone, swallowed whole by the striped wall, and so was the bedroom door. Alina wasn't trying to stop her from reaching the diary. She wasn't even trying to hurt her.

She was stopping Bee from leaving. This was a trap.

Trembling beads of sweat ran down Bee's back. *No!* This wasn't how things were going to end! Betsy Chillers didn't give up when she was down to her last soggy match and undead fish-folks had her surrounded. She didn't give up when her only way out of the vampire's cave was to keep drinking from the never-ending flask of pumpkin juice—even though it was her least favorite drink ever. And Bee wasn't going to give up now, either. *No ghost is going to get the best of me.*

"Alina, please, listen!" Bee called out as she grasped the diary.

Her fingertips barely had time to curl around the spiral spine when suddenly, as if in response, the floorboards below Bee gave way.

· 26 ·

Someone Goes Missing

Bee was falling through wisps of cobwebs and clouds of dust.

Deeper and deeper into the house.

Whispers curled around her. Air rushed past, whipping at her frizzy hair and snatching away the clips and elastics holding it together. And it felt like she was coming undone as well.

Bee was too tired to scream, too scared to look. She squeezed her eyes shut and focused on the only thing that felt real anymore—the diary against her chest. *I can't fall forever, can I?* Surely by now she'd reached the basement?

Another thought filled her head. What if there was no end to the house? What if it kept going and she kept falling, and falling, and falling . . . This was a magical house, after all, controlled by a magical and (though Bee hated to admit it) dangerous girl. Anything was possible. Bee gripped the diary so tight she felt the cover wrinkle under her fingernails. Something warm filled her mouth—blood, from where she'd accidentally split her lip.

And then it stopped. A dull light shone through a skylight above. Pillows and rolls of layered carpet were tucked under Bee. And around her, strung from the ceiling and flashing a vivid array of colors, were flowers at various stages of drying. *The clubhouse.* Bee couldn't feel the diary in her hands anymore, but she knew it was still there. She was in a memory.

Slowly she became aware of a girl sitting beside her, a girl with a thick braid of red hair and overalls and a scowl on her face. *This must be Gretta.* The door to the clubhouse opened and another girl crawled inside. Her cheeks were flushed and her hair was a dirty blond. She didn't have any freckles, but by the tilt of her nose and the length of her chin, it was obvious she and Gretta were related. The new girl sat down across from Gretta and Bee, busying herself with stringing up a bouquet of fresh flowers.

Gretta tapped her finger impatiently. "So what is it you wanted to tell me?" she asked, a bit of venom sneaking into her words. "What was so important that you couldn't say it in front of Alina?"

Bee felt herself go rigid, but the other girl didn't look up, continuing to focus on her flowers. Amid the bouquet was a single rose, and its sweet floral perfume filled the space. Finally, the girl looked up. There were streaks of dirt under her eyes, as though she'd been crying.

"Alina," she uttered, barely loud enough to hear. "That's all you talk about these days."

Gretta crossed her arms defensively. "She's my friend, my best friend. You wouldn't understand."

"Friends don't make you change who you are," the girl retorted, then stopped, her eyes flickering to either side nervously.

"I haven't changed. Sure, I've learned a few tricks, Alina's been teaching me some pretty neat stuff." Her lips curled in annoyance, and something inside Bee brightened, as though she was *enjoying* this. "But it's not my fault you're not smart, not cool enough to hang out with us, Hanna."

Bee's eyes widened as she took in the girl, as though for the first time. The soft-spoken voice, the love of flowers . . . She recalled Lucas's mom saying they had moved to Storm Lake because of school troubles, and also to be closer to her sister. Her sister, Gretta. But it wasn't some random move to a small cottaging neighborhood—Hanna had grown up here. She was just moving *back*.

Bee started to reach out, but the colors were changing and the image of the sisters was swirling together until she was alone in the clubhouse. The fresh flowers Hanna had hung up were dry now, so a few days must have gone by. A voice was calling . . . outside? Bee frowned. Wasn't this Gretta's memory? She waited and listened as the voice called out over and over again, at first from far away, but as it grew closer, Bee could pick out the strain in it, the desperation. She crawled forward and placed her ear on the door a moment before it burst open.

"Hanna?" Gretta called out. Leaves stuck out from her braid, and this time she was the one with streaks of dirt running down her cheeks. "Oh, Hanna, where are you?"

Gretta collapsed onto the nearest pile of pillows, and she looked like she might stay there and never move again. *Hanna. Hanna is missing.* Bee couldn't imagine the fear Gretta was feeling, the panic. She automatically reached out a hand to comfort her, or tried to, but she couldn't move. She was stuck in someone else's memory. Finally, after what felt like an eternity, Gretta pushed herself up and moved toward the stone wall, reaching into one of the grooves. Bee felt a chill as she recalled the juicy yellow caterpillars, but when Gretta retrieved her hand, she held only a long white candle and a plastic container—the kind her parents used to store leftovers.

Slowly, Gretta lowered the candle and stuck it firmly into the ground. Then, with a quick flick of a match, she lit the wick. The flame danced, spreading a strange warmth that prickled Bee's eyes and wrinkled her nose. Notes of clove and cinnamon and ginger enveloped her.

Then, hands shaking, Gretta opened the container and quickly brought the contents to her lips—too quickly for Bee to see. She closed her eyes. Her lips began to move quickly and the colors in the clubhouse seemed to darken ever so slightly. Bee gritted her teeth, straining to catch the words, which bled into each other like a never-ending chant.

"I-need-your-help-please-save-my-sister-I-need-your-help-please-save-my-sister."

There were three gingerbread cookies in her hands, three cookies shaped into plump bodies with long necks and pointed beaks. Was this what Gretta meant when she said the ghost had taught her some tricks? With a jolt, Bee realized her heart was beating fast and her fists were clenched, and a rising betrayal was filling her belly. Whoever's memory this was, whoever was silently watching from the shadows, was very, *very* angry.

The cookies seemed to be growing between Gretta's fingers, stretching and darkening into black-and-white feathers, until Gretta could hang on no longer. The loons burst forward one after the other from between her fingers and shot toward the plexiglass ceiling, pushing it open with a flurry of cries. As Gretta shielded her eyes, Bee caught a glimpse of the still dancing flame flickering on the wick of the candle as it was carried away in webbed feet. Toward the house across the lake.

And as the plexiglass ceiling fell to the floor, Bee caught a glimpse of herself—of long dark ringlets and porcelain features and a billowing white pirate's blouse. These weren't just anyone's memories. These were Alina's.

Bee gazed at Gretta's tearstained cheeks. Hanna had tried to warn her sister that Alina was dangerous. And like any kid who got in the way of the ghost, she had disappeared.

Bee swallowed hard. Anyone who got between Alina and her new best friend was in danger.

Lucas.

• 27 •

You Don't Belong

Bee's face was hot, too hot, like she had a terrible fever. *Lucas.* Her hands shook and her head pounded. It was exactly like the story—first the boy who bullied her, then Hanna who tried to warn her sister, and now . . . a lonely ghost who had wanted friends, stealing her enemies instead.

The diary was back in her hands, and the clubhouse's soft cushions were replaced by hard wood and bits of crumbled stone pinching her back. She was in the house again. Bee blinked back the prickly dust, waiting for her eyes to adjust to the dark. But they didn't. Carefully, she placed her hands out, feeling the too-tight confines of a room barely the size of a closet. And there was no door. Bee slid back down to the ground, holding her thumping head.

It was Bee who first wanted to see the abandoned lot, Bee who thought Alina was the coolest girl ever— so much cooler than Lucas. It was Bee who had gone back, even after all those hints that something more was afoot. And now Lucas was going to pay for her mistakes. Bee tucked the green diary into the waistband of her pants and banged the wall with her fist halfheart- edly. They were both going to be stuck here . . . forever.

From inside the closet, there were no sounds to be heard other than Bee's own breathing. She rubbed her thumb over her bracelet, but it brought little comfort. The silence was heavy, like the quiet menace of storm clouds rolling in over the lake. And behind it all, a faint scratching. Bee's head jerked up. *Scratching.* She placed an ear to the wall. *There it was!* Faint but real, starting up every few seconds. Bee shuffled around the space. When she went one way, it grew softer, but when she moved the opposite way, it grew louder. Bee stopped in front of what felt like all the other walls and listened.

The scratching was persistent, like tiny claws paw- ing at . . . With a deep breath, Bee shoved hard, and the wall trembled. But nothing else happened. She felt around with her fingers, gasping as they hooked into an outline that wasn't there before. A hidden door that Alina must have plastered over. Hope renewed, Bee took a step back, and then rushed forward, ramming her side into the wall.

With a splinter and a resounding crack, the door flew open and Bee tumbled into a hallway of flickering lights. She ran a hand hurriedly over her ribs—a bit sore, but otherwise all right—and checked to make sure her glasses were still intact.

By the looks of it, Alina and her house of horrors hadn't noticed she'd escaped. The peeling wallpaper remained still and unwavering, the floorboards didn't budge. Bee looked back at the closet she'd just broken out of and the splintered doorframe with a sniff. *Is that . . . gingerbread?* But in the next breath, the spiced scent was gone.

Something rubbed up against her leg and Bee yelped. "Albus!"

The large ginger cat brushed up against her leg again, fixing her with large, human eyes. But this time Bee wasn't creeped out. She was grateful.

"Thanks, kitty," she muttered softly, bending over to ruffle the thick fur around the cat's neck. "You knew I was in there, didn't you? That's mighty smart."

Despite Alina's attempts to trap her, Bee was okay here, for now. But where was here? The beige hallway was short, with a low ceiling that looked like it might fall through at any moment. And other than the closet she'd just broken out of, there were only three other options: three identical doors fitted with identical brass handles. Bee put a hand on the nearest one and shuddered. The metal was cold and clammy. She pulled away. Clearly, there was only one right door to open. But which one?

Albus trotted ahead of her, tail held high.

"Don't suppose you know which one will lead me to Lucas?" Bee asked, then shook her head. She'd really lost it now—talking to a cat!

But there was confidence in Albus's trot, and Bee followed her, despite her better judgment. The cat paused for a moment before standing on its hind legs and pressing both paws against the far door.

"Are you sure?"

The cat looked up and tilted its head to the side, as if to say *Do you have any better leads?* There was more to Albus than met the eye, but Bee didn't have time for another mystery. Without a second thought, she grasped the door handle and twisted.

The beige hallway disappeared as the sounds of the forest at night enveloped her. Was she still in the house? She turned, but there was no door behind her, only more forest. But not one she recognized. Instead of the straight limbs of pines, crooked trunks stretched out like the sharp angles of lightning bolts as far as she could see before melting into the darkness. An owl hooted nearby and something scurried in the undergrowth. Bee looked down.

The large ginger cat headbutted her shin and then trotted forward, skipping over the exposed gnarled roots of black locust trees. Their white flowers hung from the branches like eerie, tiny moons. Bee looked around, hoping for a clue as to where she was, but the forest was dark and, as far as she could tell, went on forever. A cold light emanated from above, the same light as the flickering bulb in the hallway. There were no stars. Bee wasn't sure how it was possible, but despite appearances, she was still in Alina's house.

Bee watched as Albus bounded ahead of her—the fluff ball seemed to know where to go, and Bee followed. The trees were getting more and more crooked, the branches zigzagging at odd angles with the round bellies of boulders breaking the earth now and again. This definitely wasn't the forest around Storm Lake. *Why did Alina build this room?* Bee followed the ginger cat tentatively, making sure not to trip over any roots. Every few meters, Albus would stop and look back as if she, too, was concerned, before skipping ahead again. After a few minutes, the trees thinned, and Bee's bare feet felt the rough surface of asphalt.

The chime of bells started up and colorful lights blinked on a little ways ahead, and the dark shapes she'd assumed to be more boulders and trees revealed themselves. Bee gasped. She'd only seen the advertisements a million times with Kitty: the Ferris Wheel of Impending Doom, the Roller Coaster of Ghosts You Can Never Unsee, the Try-It-If-You-Dare Scream Drop. The Betsy Chillers amusement park she'd wanted so badly to go to with her friend instead of spending the week at the cottage with her family.

It was all right there, right in front of her, abandoned in the middle of the forest. Bee shook her head. No, created by Alina in one of the rooms of her magic house. *This isn't real.* Bee continued forward, weaving under the dark shadows of the rides, jumping a low fence, and stealing past an empty cotton candy stall. It was quiet, the way no real amusement park ever would be. And then Bee heard it; a soft giggle floating on the wind. She gritted her teeth and returned her attention to Albus; the cat knew exactly where she was going.

The giggles grew louder as Bee and Albus wove their way deeper into the park, putting every nerve in Bee's body on edge. What was it about that particular sound? Wasn't giggling simply a close cousin of laughing? But there was nothing funny about the way the voices coiled around her ears like the whine of mosquitoes, teased her like an invisible hand tapping on her shoulder, daring her to look, hummed into her chest until it felt like that's where the giggles were coming from—from *inside*. Bee took a deep breath and forced her feet to keep moving—Betsy Chillers had been in worse situations than this, and she never gave up.

It's not real.

The outline of a merry-go-round loomed before Bee, unmoving in the dark, as though waiting for something. And assembled around it, the unmistakable silhouettes of a crowd. Just standing there.

Bee crouched behind a toy vending machine stacked

with large-eyed bobblehead versions of Betsy Chillers, and watched as Albus wove her way through the legs of the crowd. There was the chatter of children, giggling in groups of twos and threes, pointing at something Bee couldn't see. There were adults, too, talking in mocking tones, snickering and whispering to each other.

"Albus!" A relieved voice cut through the rest, and Bee's heart pounded.

She stood, backing up to get a better view of the ride, and sure enough, there he was. Unmistakable with his flash of red hair and goggles and, now, with Albus back around his shoulders, Lucas sat immobile on one of the aluminum ponies, feet firmly strapped into the stirrups and hands clamped onto the pole rising out of the pony's spine. *He's all right!*

But he wasn't free.

Bee stepped forward, closer to the crowd, huddling her arms beneath the life jacket. What was Alina trying to prove? Was it as simple as walking up there and helping Lucas? Knowing the ghost, there was always something more. A girl with blond hair and a pinched expression turned as Bee approached. She wore a frilly new pink shirt and a sparkly choker.

Bee stopped in her tracks. It didn't make sense—it was impossible—and yet there she was. The all too familiar blue eyes that always held a hint of laughter; the light bounciness in the way she flicked her wrists and smiled, pulling everyone around her a little closer as though popularity held its own gravity. It had to be her.

"Kitty?" Bee stuttered. "What are you doing here?"

"What do you mean, what am *I* doing here?" Kitty smirked. "You're the one who doesn't belong, or did you forget?"

She gestured to the kids behind her, other classmates Bee recognized from school, as well as the two new friends she'd seen in the picture from Kitty's trip to the amusement park. *New day, new friends.* Like a single well-dressed, too-cool-for-school organism, their eyes turned to slits and their nostrils flared as they focused on Bee.

Bee stepped back. Kitty would never say that, would she? She searched Kitty's face for a hint of a smile, anything to say this was all a joke, a misunderstanding. But Kitty didn't back down.

"What are you talking about? We're friends, aren't we?" Bee's voice trembled. "We read Betsy Chillers together and go to the same swimming lessons."

"Sure, but it's not like I'd ever hang out with you at, say, a bookstore after school," Kitty said.

Bee swallowed hard.

"Even if it means missing out on a signed copy of *Betsy Chillers*. Some things aren't worth it." Kitty rolled her eyes. "Like being seen with someone who wears hand-me-downs."

"But . . ." Bee frowned. "You said you liked my style, that it's vintage."

Kitty pinched her nose. "And packs spicy pickles for their lunch all the time."

Bee stepped back again, lip trembling. "My mom stopped packing that in my lunch box ages ago!"

"And has a weirdo family."

Bee's breath hitched. She'd always thought of her family as weird. But hearing someone else say it . . .

Kitty's lip curled. "You're just embarrassing, and you don't belong here."

It felt like a wave smacking into her chest. Bee couldn't breathe. Couldn't talk. Couldn't look at Kitty for one more second. She turned, rushing back to the safety of the vending machine's shadow. She squeezed her eyes shut and slid down its side, her chest aching. Kitty and her friends didn't follow her. Through the ringing in her ears, she could hear their jeering and gig-gling starting up around Lucas again.

She knew it wasn't real; it couldn't be. It looked like Kitty, but if she focused hard enough, there were subtle differences: the voice was a bit higher, the brows too pinched. The crowd was like the orange-and-pink flames in the fireplace—fake. But it still hurt, because deep down, she knew Kitty's words were also a little bit true.

After all, her friend always did have a not-so-nice comment or two about Bee's cousin's hand-me-downs. And she had never showed up at that bookstore, mak-ing Bee feel bad, when it had been Kitty's idea in the first place. And Kitty didn't like any food Bee's parents made and wasn't afraid to let everyone know, even if it was Bee's birthday. Somehow Alina's house wasn't just good at pulling out all her dreams and wishes; it was also very good at pulling out Bee's worst nightmares.

Bee tried to push herself up, but her legs felt as heavy as stone blocks and her chest tightened, and there wasn't anything she could do about it. Alina was going to win. She was going to get everything she wanted. And Lucas and Bee were never going to leave.

· 28 ·

The Light

You're just embarrassing. Bee squeezed her eyes shut again, waiting for the ringing in her ears to stop. A cold breeze swept through the amusement park, covering her skin in goose bumps. How could just a few words be so hurtful? Words she had said almost verbatim to her mom the last time they spoke. *A weirdo family.* Bee hugged her knees close, regret coloring her cheeks.

She thought of her parents and all their quirks, waking up in an empty cottage, wondering where she'd gone. Was it really so bad that her mom liked a good deal and didn't care what others thought of her morning dock yoga routine? Was it so bad that her dad liked to holler before cannonballing into the lake like no one was watching?

All this time, Bee had wished she could be more like Kitty, more like Alina, so she could fit in. Maybe there was another way.

Bee peered at the crowd again, and at Lucas sitting there at its center, petting Albus and waiting quietly, doing a fabulous job of ignoring the laughing.

"Why isn't he hurting, too?" she muttered.

Didn't he care that they were making fun of him? But Bee already knew Lucas wasn't one to care about fitting in. *Maybe that's why he's not being affected.*

Bee's jaw clenched. A few lightbulbs pulsed on and off around the roof of the merry-go-round, bouncing a gray light off the porcelain ponies, casting shadows over Albus's ginger fur. *Betsy Chillers's fourth rule of thumb: Never give up.*

But for once, Betsy Chillers didn't make Bee feel better. Instead, she thought of someone else. Someone who was always strong for her family, who sometimes burned the chapatis and often hummed off-key, and, most important, would never have changed who she was—not for anything in the world. *Granny.*

And what was it that Granny always said? It wasn't always about appearances and something about the heart? Bee tried to remember and her eyes prickled all over again. She brought her bracelet to her cheek, wiping away the tears.

Gingerly Bee got to her feet and stepped out into the open. The chatter and laughing from Kitty and her friends stopped all at once, and a dozen pairs of eyes fixed on her.

Bee's heart pounded as she willed herself to walk, but Kitty stepped forward to block her.

Her face stretched into a scowl. "You're still here? I thought I told you to leave!"

Bee steadied her voice. *She's not real. This isn't real.* "Not without Lucas."

Kitty crossed her arms, flipping back her silky hair. "So now you're hanging out with weirdos that wear goggles?"

"He's not a weirdo." Bee's heart drummed faster and faster, like rain hitting the cottage roof.

Kitty let out a sharp laugh. "Wait a second. Maybe you can't tell, because you're exactly the same." She paused, looking Bee up and down. "Just admit it, you're a weirdo, too."

Bee's neck was hot and her heart felt like it might fly out of her chest. Kitty was right. But she was also wrong. Sure, her dad spewed fun facts at the dinner table and her family ate dosa on special occasions. Maybe those weren't "normal" things to Kitty; maybe they were a bit different to a family who didn't ever have to think about money and had lived in the same place for generations. But they were normal to Bee, and she was tired of feeling bad about it.

The wind blew through the amusement park, but it didn't bring a chill. This time, it brought words.

"*Beauty is not in the face; beauty is the light in the heart*," a familiar voice whispered. Bee turned around, searching the dark angles of the rides.

"Granny?" she whispered.

"Admit it." Kitty stepped forward, coming so close Bee could see the frown lines in her forehead. "You don't fit in."

Bee took a deep breath, pushing past her, and was surprised to find there was no resistance. Just a cold, cold mist that sank into her skin and filled her stomach with a deep pit of emptiness. A pit of longing that had followed her ever since she had first set eyes on Alina. Or maybe it had been there long before that, too. Bee shook her head, pushing forward through the shapes of the crowd, which seemed to grow in size in front of her eyes.

"*You don't fit in.*" The whispers kept building as Bee pushed forward, catching glimpses of Kitty's laughing face and silky hair. "*You don't fit in.*"

She wasn't far now—the merry-go-round was only a few footsteps away.

"You don't fit in." A girl turned to block her way, hands on her hips.

Bee nearly stopped, wavering. This wasn't just any friend of Kitty's. The girl in front of her had frizzy hair that still glistened from a recent dip in the lake, and thick-rimmed glasses perched on a blotchy face, and pants that floated a bit too high off the ground. *Is that*

252

really what I look like? Is that really me?

"You don't fit in," the girl repeated, pushing up her glasses.

Bee gritted her teeth. "Get out of my way!"

The girl held her gaze, grinning. And then Bee realized something.

She didn't need to look like someone else or eat different food or hang out with friends who didn't really care about her, just to fit in. Bee stared at the girl's frizzy hair, which actually looked quite impressive, like the mane of some majestic night creature. She took in the skin, which tanned so beautifully under the summer sun. Then she looked past the glasses, deep into the girl's dazzling brown eyes . . . and smiled. *Actually, I like the way I look.*

The girl's grin faded to confusion.

Then Bee took a breath and ran forward through the ghost of herself, ignoring the cold that seeped into her bones, ignoring the tightness in her chest. Barely noticing the pit in her stomach that had finally started to shrink. She didn't stop until her hands met the wooden platform of the merry-go-round.

She'd done it. She had actually done it. Bee allowed herself a very brief, very small smile.

"You're here, thank goodness!" Lucas cried.

In his excitement and relief, he attempted to jump off the pony, but his feet remained stuck to the stirrups as though tied by invisible rope. "Ouch!" he yelped.

It was a beautiful merry-go-round, the glistening ponies painted to look quasi-realistic with chestnut-brown fur and dark manes and taupe leather harnesses. The floorboards were painted a bright green to mimic grassy fields, and the intricately carved pavilion showcased a multitude of blues, swirling together into a picture-perfect sky, a stark contrast to the starless sky above them.

"It was all thanks to Albus. She led me right to you," Bee said, giving the cat a nod (she'd come a long way in her thinking about cats). "Here, keep still while I take a look." She gestured to his feet.

"I was following Alina, or at least I thought I was," Lucas chattered as Bee tried to free him. "But then I ended up here, walking through this abandoned theme park. I spotted this ride and just felt I had to try it out. It was weird, like there was something pulling me toward it. But once I sat on this pony thing, I couldn't get back off."

Bee stood. "What do you mean, 'abandoned,' there's a huge crowd . . ." She stopped, realizing how silent things had become the moment she stepped onto the merry-go-round platform.

"Oh, look! I'm unstuck!"

Bee turned just as the platform jerked under her feet.

"Ah!" she yelled, falling into Lucas as he dismounted.

The merry-go-round was starting to spin. Lucas grew quiet as they turned, observing the crowd of silent people going by over and over again. They weren't laughing anymore—they weren't even moving.

"They weren't there before, were they?" he asked nervously.

Bee gripped the pole for support as the merry-go-round spun faster. The crowd was blurring together, staring at her with big hollow eyes. Her heart hammered in her ears as wind tore at her hair and they spun faster and faster, until the crowed blended into a single figure with large eyes and brown ringlets, grinning with the sharpness of freshly honed hedge trimmers. *Alina.*

"We have to jump off! Bee!"

Lucas was yelling, shaking her shoulder, but she couldn't tear her eyes away from the beautiful face, as seamless as the painted ponies. The wind roared in her ears. *Stay with me. Stay with me and you'll really belong. Here you can be perfect.*

Bee tried to look away but couldn't. And the more she looked, the more she saw. Alina's skin flaked away in patches of ash. The hair on her scalp lifted as though by some invisible wind, coiling around her head like snakes. Her jaw appeared broken, hanging precariously down by her collarbones. Alina was changed, like the house, into something broken.

Or maybe that's how she had really been all along.

Alina's mouth opened wider, and it was a dark hole with no end. The more Bee stared, the more she felt like she was falling forward into it. She reached out, shuffled forward, stumbled.

"Bee!"

The strong waft of gingerbread smacked her in the nose and Bee ripped her eyes away, back to Lucas and his fantastic red hair. As red as the pony's beady eye. *Wait a second.* The pony winked, the smooth painted surface transforming into sleek black feathers and a white speckled neck until it wasn't a pony at all. The loon stood guard in front of them protectively, wings outstretched. And then another voice cut through the wind.

"Hey, you! Leave her alone!"

Bee looked back just in time to see a blur of pink tackle Alina from the side. *What was that?*

But there was no time to stop. Lucas grabbed Bee's hand and they jumped. Bee hit the asphalt first, rolling and then crouching. She was no longer spinning, but the world still was. Alina was on the ground, too, holding her head and looking dazed.

"Let's go!" Someone pulled her by the elbow. Someone. And it wasn't Lucas, who was scrambling to his feet in front of her.

Bee's breath hitched as she swiveled and came face-to-face with the last person she expected to see, and somehow the person she needed most: Granny, with her wide-brimmed pink sun hat and her eyes unclouded and her grip strong. *How?* The question hung on the edge of Bee's lips as she jumped to her feet.

And then before she could say anything, they were running (yes, even Granny! Turns out she had another speed after all).

Lucas was already ahead of them, following the loon's black flapping wings and echoing call. It bounced off the metal of the amusement park rides and then off the walls that made up the sky and surrounded the forest.

Bee's heart thumped and her breath came out in short puffs as the three of them raced into the shelter of the black locust forest, leaping over the gnarled roots and ducking under the moon-shaped flowers. Something crashed behind them, and it sounded like thunder.

"There!" Granny cried.

The outline of a white door gleamed between the trees like a sliver of moonlight, practically invisible. It flung itself open at their approach. The loon flew through first, leading them into the beige corridor, which seemed to melt at its approach, and down a newly formed staircase. They raced forward, not daring to look back, not daring to slow down.

The front door opened ahead, letting in the crack of thunder. The wind screamed through the pines and rain slanted sideways, pelting through the door. The storm big enough to scare adults had finally arrived. But it didn't scare Bee. Her chest swelled with relief as rain reached her skin and streaked her glasses, as her eyes took in the dark, angry sky and the tree line waving madly. Because this was real—they were going to make it out of the house. Lucas and Granny burst outside first. *We made it! We made it!*

But then something caught Bee's recently healed ankle. Pain sprang up her leg and she tripped, falling face-first into the entryway. *No!* Bee rolled onto her back to face Alina, breathing hard as the ghost yanked her foot again, drawing her closer.

"Where do you think you're going?"

· 29 ·

A Storm Is Called

Bee gritted her teeth as Alina dug her fingernails into her skin. Her mouth was drawn into a snarl and her hair circled her head like wild snakes.

"I know you," Alina hissed, and try as she might, Bee could no longer see the girl she used to look up to. Thunder rolled in from outside, shaking her to the bone. "You want to be cool like Kitty. You want to fit in. And I can give you those things. Stay here with me! Choose me!"

Bee kicked out, but Alina held on tight, and the green diary slid out of Bee's waistband and onto the ground. A darkness flickered near the hallway carpet, dancing like a sliver of flame that had crawled out of the fireplace.

"We're the same, you and me. All I wanted was to have friends, but the other kids, they hated me. They kept pushing me away, further and further. So I did what I had to do to keep them close."

Bee's mouth filled with bitterness, her stomach churning. Was that what had really happened? Alina hadn't noticed it yet, the dark fire that was inching its way forward, licking the wallpaper and turning it to ash. But there was no heat, no smoke. This wasn't any normal fire. This wasn't fire at all. *It's a memory!*

Her first day on Storm Lake, her dad had said something about the abandoned lot. That it had burned down in a terrible fire. Something about a kid's prank. But was it? Alina's face elongated as her mouth stretched open farther in a cry.

"Please don't leave me here alone like they did! Don't betray me! Be my friend!"

Bee remembered how desperate Gretta had been to keep Hanna safe. How she'd asked the loons for help. And how they'd flown away with a single burning candle toward the abandoned lot. Bee gasped. *She never meant to hurt Alina. She was only trying to protect her sister.* And that was the truth.

The flame grabbed hold of Alina's foot and she screeched, as though it burned right through her. As though she was living that night all over again. The loons' calls floated over the lake, the sound drawing closer and closer. The black fire had reached the ceiling now, its tendrils grasping at the ghost.

This was Bee's chance. With a tremendous effort, she twisted out of Alina's grip, using arms strengthened from all the canoeing to pull herself away. She panted at the entrance, meeting Alina's gaze.

"That's not how you make friends," Bee breathed. "And *they* didn't betray you—you betrayed them, remember? I love my family; I love myself. And I would never give those up."

Feathers flew as the loons rushed into the entrance and straight at Alina, flapping their large wings and calling out to each other. Pushing her back into the dark fire. Bee wasn't sure what was real and what was memory anymore, but the green diary was nowhere to be seen.

She crawled over the threshold of the front door into the rain, then climbed to her feet and stumbled forward, dazed, as behind her the cottage raged in a cold inferno. *Don't look back.* Bee ran down the wet grassy slope, knees shaking as she tried not to slip and fall. *Don't look back.* It was a short distance to the cobblestone path, but it felt like forever. *Don't look back.*

By the time Bee reached the water's edge, the rain had stopped completely. The wind was calming down now, and patches of sky broke through the clouds. She gasped, finding her breath. And then gasped again as she looked up. Trails of light streaked across the sky, blinking and twinkling as they connected with the lake's reflection. The meteor shower her dad had been waiting for—the ultimate light show.

Lucas was still untying the canoe, and Granny was sitting at the front in her flannel nightie, her white hair almost glowing under the full moon. There was no sign of the peach pickle barrier along the shoreline, washed away by the storm.

"Granny!" Bee clambered into the canoe and fell into her.

Granny wrapped her arms around Bee. The scariness of what had just happened, the fear, the danger, suddenly hit Bee, and she melted into Granny's embrace. Tears rolled down her cheeks as Granny stroked her hair.

"There, there, it's all right."

Her voice was as soothing as Bee remembered it being during grade school, back when Kitty's words still stung, before she learned to laugh with her classmates.

"How did you know I was here? How did you manage to save us?" Bee asked, pulling back and drying her eyes. She thought about how Granny had been around less and less lately, how she disappeared in the evenings. "I thought you were gone."

"I have a good nose for trouble, so I just followed the bread crumbs." Granny smiled, her clear eyes crinkling.

Bee observed her, the features strange but familiar,

elegant but strong. A lot of things had changed in the past year.

"Um, Bee?" Lucas cleared his throat. His gaze swept across Granny confusedly. "I don't mean to interrupt, but maybe we should get going."

Bee pulled away, reaching for an oar. But Granny put a hand on her arm, stopping her.

"No," she said.

"Granny, what are you doing?" Bee asked. "We have to go!"

But Granny held firm. "No. You have to make things right with Alina. Otherwise, this will happen again, to another you and another Lucas."

Bee stared at her. "But there was a huge fire! I can't go back in there!"

"What fire?" Granny asked calmly.

Bee frowned, peering back through the pines, expecting to see those black flames reaching for the trees. There was only silence, punctuated by the chirping of crickets and toads.

"Everyone has fears, something they're scared of. Even Alina." Granny gestured back to Bee's chest, where the light from the passing meteors flickered against the life jacket's buckle, making it look like a small, pulsing star. "But she can't hurt you anymore, remember? You know who you are."

Granny was right. Bee had come here for a reason— to find the last bread crumb and help Alina. And she'd discovered the truth, about Hanna and Gretta, and about how the fire had really started. Now it was time for the second part.

Bee steadied herself, taking long, deep breaths. *I know who I am.* But that still didn't make it any easier.

And then she made her way out of the canoe and back onto shore. Toward the waiting ghost of Storm Lake.

· 30 ·

You'll Like This Deal

For once, there was no Betsy Chillers rule of thumb to lean on. Bee walked forward, focusing on putting one foot after the other instead of on what lay ahead. Easier said than done, though, when all she could picture was Alina with her unhooked jaw, screaming at the top of her ghostly lungs as black fire enveloped her. Bee shuddered. What had Lucas's aunt said, again? *The more you wish you weren't so different, the more you wish you could fit in, the more Alina's power will continue to grow.*

Bee took a deep breath. She knew that she belonged now. With her parents, with Granny, and with Lucas. But would that be enough for Alina?

She stopped at the front door—or where the front

door should have been. The skeleton of the house, with its cracked marble countertops and moss-covered floors and charred walls, stood quietly in the night, as though the memory of the fire had drained both Alina and the house of their magic—their strength. It was just a pile of rubble, just as it had been since it was abandoned decades ago.

Not rubble. . . . Bee brought a piece of plaster to her face and sniffed. *Gingerbread!* She picked through the crumbling stone and baby ferns and ash.

"Alina?" she called out tentatively. Twigs snapped under her feet. "Alina, are you here?"

She quieted her breathing, listening to the whining mosquitoes and the wind in the trees. A single sob. It was muffled and distant, but there was no mistaking it. Bee walked toward the sound, past the old fireplace and into the kitchen.

The cast-iron stove was blackened with age but still standing. One of the few things the fire hadn't destroyed. Cautiously, she lifted the heavy handle and let the door swing outward.

"What are you doing here?" the ghost screamed, covering her face. Dark lines streaked her cheeks, tears mixed with ash. "Did you come to gloat?"

Bee stumbled back. "No, no, never," she stuttered.

Alina looked so innocent, so sad tucked into the oven. With her glistening eyes and hair as dark and flowing as the goddess Kali's. And just as dangerous.

But like Kali, there was a place for Alina in this world, too. At least, that's what Granny believed. It was what Bee believed, too. She reached inside and grasped Alina's hand.

"I came to make sure you were okay," Bee said.

Alina wiped her eyes with the back of her sleeve and took Bee's hand. She then slid herself onto the stovetop, legs swinging anxiously, and Bee was reminded why she had gone back across the lake, despite Gretta's warning. Alina was a ghost, but she was also just a kid like Bee. A lonely kid who wanted to fit in.

"Also," Bee said, "to tell you that I'm going home soon."

"Oh." Alina looked away, and Bee thought she saw a glimmer of genuine sadness in her face. "Oh well, plenty of other options to choose from, I guess, as long as that *witch* stays out of my way."

She fixed Bee with her round, dark eyes, but there was something in her voice that told Bee she felt differently. Gretta's words came back to her. *Who do you think was the first kid Alina tried to trap?*

"That fire . . ." Bee hesitated. "That fire was a memory. But I don't think it was on purpose. Gretta was trying to protect her sister; they were afraid of you."

"Gretta." Alina's jaw tightened. "She came to me— canoed across the lake just like you did. We were friends, and I taught her everything she knows."

Bee's heartbeat quickened as she thought of the dough under Gretta's fingernails as she biked down the steep gravel road, of the clandestine meetings with Alina at night, and of the loons. The same way Gretta could turn gingerbread cookies into real loons, Alina had made a gingerbread house—a house that came alive at night and lured in children from across the lake. *Gingerbread magic.*

Alina opened her mouth in a slow grimace. "And it was a big mistake." Then she turned to the side and spat. "We were getting along so well until her little sister started to whisper things behind my back. She thought I was dangerous, thought I was changing Gretta and that I would hurt her."

"But you *were* changing Gretta," Bee argued. *The same way I was changing, too—into someone who lied to her parents and said mean things to people she cared about.* "And you *did* hurt Hanna. She got lost in the woods, remember? And weren't you planning on keeping Gretta with you in your house forever? That sounds kind of dangerous to me."

"I—" Alina's mouth twisted into something that looked like a pout, and her eyebrows slanted with a mixture of confusion and sadness. And maybe regret. But it was so fleeting, Bee couldn't be sure. "Whatever," Alina huffed. "That witch was never my friend. She's been using my own magic against me ever since, always keeping an eye on things with those horrid gingerbread loons of hers."

Bee wrapped her arms around herself, a lump in her throat. She felt bad for Alina, abandoned by the town and then abandoned by her friend. But Alina was also dangerous, even if she didn't realize it.

"I understand what it's like, wanting to fit in. . . ." Bee hesitated. "I had a hard time making friends, too."

Alina grinned. "I know all about Kitty, remember?"

Bee looked down. "Right." *You used my insecurities against me.* On second thought, it was difficult to feel bad for someone who'd recently attempted to trap you in a magic house for all eternity.

"But it doesn't have to be like that. . . ." Bee trailed off as Alina stuck her nose in the air.

This is going to be harder than I thought. It was time to put everything on the table.

"You want to have a friend, don't you? You don't want to be alone anymore? I think there's something I can do about that . . . I want to propose a deal. A truce."

Alina threw herself forward off the stovetop, landing lightly on the ground. "I don't *do* deals."

This was it. She was either going to go for it, or she wasn't. The hauntings on Storm Lake were either going to stop forever, or . . .

Bee felt her neck prickle. "What if I can prove you

wrong? What if I can show you that Gretta really was your friend? That the sisters did care about you?"

Alina raised a delicate eyebrow. "You can try."

The moment the canoe left land, the chill that had enveloped Bee for the past few hours faded; her shoulders relaxed and her breath evened out. They had made it. She'd done it. Lucas was safe, and although she still wasn't sure where the diary had gone, things with Alina were . . . better. And yet . . . Bee felt the tug of the braided bracelet around her wrist and a twinge of sadness plucked at her heartstrings.

Granny's silhouette was barely visible at the front of the canoe. And sometimes, when Bee blinked, it wasn't there at all.

"I wish you weren't so sad," Granny said as Bee dipped the paddle into the sparkling water, long streaks flashing through the sky as stars arced across. "I wish you'd be proud instead."

"Proud?" Bee quickly wiped a tear that slid down her cheek between paddle strokes. "What are you saying? *You* saved the day, Granny. If it wasn't for you—"

"Nonsense. It was all you, my dear," Granny said. "Why are you still crying?"

Bee sniffled quietly, unable to stop the tears. They had waited a long time to come out, after all. At first, after Granny passed away, it felt as though things could stay the same. Bee would wake up and Granny would still be there, sitting in her usual spot at the table for breakfast. When she'd come home from school after a rough day, Granny would be waiting for her in the kitchen, just like before.

But lately, things had changed. Lately, there were times when she wasn't there—like in the evenings when Bee was supposed to be sleeping, or on long afternoons at the cottage. In those moments, it was as though she was slowly slipping away from Bee's thoughts. And she was scared that one day, Granny would disappear altogether. Thankfully, though, that hadn't happened yet. Granny was still here.

The ghost that was Granny gestured to the braided bracelet on Bee's wrist. The bracelet she'd made just for Bee almost a year ago now.

"It's just . . . ," Bee started, the words sticking to her throat like sticky-sweet jalebi. "Now that everything is all right and I'm safe, what if I don't see you again? What if you think I don't need you anymore?"

Bee's chest was tight. Too tight. Because the truth was, she would always need her granny. She was sure of it.

"It's okay to feel that way." Granny's voice was quiet now. So quiet, Bee had to hold her breath to hear it. "You may not always see me as easily in the future, but there are others you can count on. There are others who will stand beside you when things get . . . complicated, as you say."

"Who?"

"Your family and your friends! Your true friends, that is." Granny glanced at Lucas. "And anyway, I'll always be here." She laid a hand gently on Bee's chest, above her heart. "As long as you need me."

The last tear dripped off Bee's chin and onto her knee.

"Beautiful." The silhouette shimmered, and it seemed as though Granny was tilting her head to the sky.

"The meteor shower is beautiful, yes." Bee frowned, then inhaled sharply. "Wait, you can see the lights?"

"Only the important ones," she replied slyly. And then the canoe swayed a bit before righting itself, as Granny turned away from Bee, hiding a knowing smile.

The paddle back was quiet, the lake completely still after the storm, as if it were taking a long, restful sleep. Bee stifled the beginnings of a yawn.

"I feel bad for Alina, in a way," Lucas said. "I think it's a good thing you wanted to keep that last bread crumb from my auntie. She's just lonely, and I don't think being trapped in that house forever is going to make things any better."

Bee nodded in agreement as they approached the dock, thinking about her deal with Alina—her truce. And hoping very hard that she was doing the right thing.

The canoe secured, they climbed onto the dock and Bee stood for a moment at its edge, watching the meteor shower. A series of coos alerted Bee to the three loons, who, she was happy to see, had also made it back in one piece. They wove in and out of the cattails, before continuing along the lake's perimeter.

"Hey." Lucas nudged her arm. "Who were you talking to back there, in the canoe?"

Bee glanced at Granny, still sitting happily in the canoe—a canoe that Bee knew was completely empty. But admitting that, saying those words out loud . . . Her chest tightened and she bit her lip.

"My . . . um—"

Albus suddenly leaped from Lucas's arms onto Bee's shoulders.

"Hey!" Lucas tsked at his cat. "Who said you could do that?"

"No, it's all right, actually," Bee said, petting the soft fur for the first time and feeling the comforting weight pressed against her shoulders.

And it was. Lucas stood beside her, close enough that she could feel the warmth coming off his arm, and Albus purred soothingly, and it felt like everything was right with the world.

· 31 ·

Granny's Celebration

Bee woke up early on the day of the party, as soon as the birds began their morning chorus. She prepared egg paratha (with an added dollop of ghee for extra crispiness) for her pleasantly surprised parents, then went for a long walk along the gravel path (this time when she got to the end of the driveway, she turned left).

"Aren't you spry," her mother commented when Bee got back. Mrs. Bakshi was donning her special occasion purple-and-gold sari. "I hope you kept your promise about taking care of the invitations."

She ran a finger down her list of dishes (Mrs. Bakshi enjoyed making lists; it gave her a special satisfaction to cross the items off one by one) and cranked on the stove.

"Don't worry, I did." Bee smiled, rolling up her sleeves to wash a bowl of potatoes.

By "I," of course, Bee meant herself and Lucas, who, it turned out, was very good at making small talk with the neighbors and turning even the most squiggly-inducing activities into an almost fun afternoon. Almost.

The screen door creaked as her dad came into the house, dripping wet with lake water.

"You'll never guess what I saw on the lake," he said excitedly. "A snapping turtle! And it was this big." He gestured in the air with his hands. "Did you know their mouths are powerful beaks that can snap your finger like a carrot?"

"No way!" Bee gasped.

"Watch the floor, don't get it wet!" her mom fretted, throwing the closest towel she could find across the kitchen to him. "And weren't you supposed to go help the other neighbors with that fallen tree?"

Last night's storm had been just as violent as the weather forecast predicted, albeit several days late. Some of the cottages lost a few shingles off their roofs, and any inflatable water toys were as good as gone, swept up by the winds and torrential rains. Even a few trees got uprooted, but luckily only one landed on anything significant.

"Oh yes, we did that first," Bee's dad said. "That storage shed was completely smashed, but we did our best packing up anything that was salvageable! Sweaty

275

business, so thought I'd cool off afterward."

Bee and her mom shared a look—they both knew Mr. Bakshi would find any excuse to sneak in a swim. He walked by the table, seeing if there were any snacks ready to grab, and chuckled at the freshly prepped carrots.

"Also, you wouldn't believe what I just heard," Mr. Bakshi said, taking a crunchy bite. "Apparently, that meteor shower happened last night, and we missed it! That big storm completely covered up the sky! Such bad luck."

"Oh, you don't say." Her mom clicked her tongue against the roof of her mouth. "So rare, a once-in-a-lifetime thing . . . It would have been magical, huh, Binita?"

Bee smiled to herself, wishing Lucas were around to share in their little secret.

But there was lots to do and little time to do it, so as soon as Bee finished cutting up all the vegetables, she was outside dragging plastic chairs around the kitchen table. The party would take place in the yard, with a perfect view of the lake.

Perfect, everything's perfect. From the gold balloons floating from the deck and chairs to the bunches of sunflowers Mrs. Bakshi had found at the market. Bee adjusted the frilly orange top that she'd chosen in lieu of Alina's blue silk romper (although the blue romper was exquisite . . . maybe another time). And every so often she'd stop to look up, her gaze wandering to the other side of the lake and the abandoned lot.

At one o'clock sharp, the guests began to arrive.

"Bee!" Lucas waved, dressed in slightly more formal sweatpants than usual. There was something different about him.

She stifled a laugh. "Your hair—you brushed it."

Lucas passed a hand over his mostly coiffed locks, which were having a hard time maintaining their partition. A few curls were already bouncing stubbornly back into place. Even Albus looked like a comb had been passed over her thick coat.

"You guys look good," Bee assured him, before turning to greet the others.

Hanna was already inside, helping Mrs. Bakshi carry the remaining dishes to the table, while Gretta offered Mr. Bakshi a platter of cookies. She was back in her long brown overcoat, and her hair hid most of her face. If Gretta stood still for long enough, she could easily be mistaken for a tree stump (ideal for keeping a close eye on ghosts and such), and Bee decided it was a rather practical fashion choice in the end.

Bee stiffened as Gretta's eyes found hers. Was she angry about their trip back across the lake? Would she reprimand Bee for not heeding her warning?

"These look . . . so interesting," her dad commented. "What kind of cookies are these?"

"Gingerbread," Gretta said. "Family recipe."

Then she threw Bee a wink that felt a lot like *I knew what you were planning the entire time—I'm a witch, remember; nothing gets past me.* And Bee let out a breath of relief.

It was odd, knowing Gretta had once been friends with Alina, and what she had done to keep her sister safe. But then again, there was nothing Bee wouldn't have done to save Lucas. And nothing would ever have stopped Granny from rescuing the both of them.

As Auntie Gretta took Lucas aside for a serious-sounding chat, the final guests arrived—Eli and his parents, each wearing a "Happy Valley Peaches Farm" baseball cap of their own and holding a basket of fresh, juicy peaches. And then Bee's mom came out in her beautiful gold-and-purple sari, the large frilly card in her hands, and everyone fell into a comfortable silence.

"Thank you for coming," she said, dark hair framing the beginnings of a sad frown. "If my mother were with us, she would be interrupting me right about now for a glass of water or a cup of tea." She chuckled, dabbing the edges of her eyes with a napkin. "She always did have the worst timing in those things. But the best timing for what really mattered."

Bee's chest tightened as her mom continued, gazing at the sad faces around her.

"You ready, Binita?" her dad asked, holding the card over the firepit.

Slowly Bee walked over to take his place.

"Big card for big feelings," he whispered, before kissing her forehead and striking the match.

The paper caught instantly, the flames swallowing up the ink and the glitter as it fell into the firepit in a ball of light.

"Your granny would have loved this," Bee's mom concluded. "Having her cottaging friends gathered together, being merry and remembering her."

A warm tear slipped down Bee's cheek, and she brought her hand up.

"What are you crying for?" Granny leaned in beside her, a crown of dried yellow flowers on her head. "I'll always be with you, remember?"

Bee met Lucas's gaze as another tear slid down her face.

"Right next to that light," Granny said, and for a second, Bee felt something warm against her chest, right across her heart. "Okay?"

Bee nodded, drying her eyes. "Okay."

And then, the moment everybody was waiting for. Bee's dad brought his hands together in a loud clap. "Time to eat!"

All in all, it was a perfect day. The weather held up, her parents' cooking received rave reviews, and for the first time in a while, Bee's appetite returned—she could taste every delicious swirl of ghee in her mother's vegetable curry, every scrumptious spice in the biryani.

It was so perfect, Bee wondered how she could ever have been so scared—far from seeing them as weird, everyone adored her family. Eli's parents even invited them to their annual fall harvest BBQ the next month.

"Bee." Hanna came to sit down beside her as guests trickled back down the gravel driveway. She wore a flowery summer dress that trailed in the grass when she walked. "I wanted to give you something. A little thank-you."

She placed a gift bag on the table and slid it over, smiling.

"Lucas has had such a good week, and it's because of you. I wanted you to know I'm grateful."

Bee frowned, peeking into the gift bag. "Oh, you don't have to give me anything. He's the cool one, and I'm happy he let me hang out with—OH!"

She held the hardcover to her face in disbelief. Betsy Chillers number forty-three.

"The exclusive release you can only get at the amusement park!" Bee stuttered, turning it over in her hands. "Thank you so much!"

"Your mom and I got to talking, and she mentioned you were a fan." Hanna chuckled. "Plus, being the author has its perks."

She picked at a leftover samosa while Bee passed a hand over the glossy cover, showcasing the one and only Betsy Chillers in the throes of a monster hunt, with her familiar ruffled pirate shirt and glossy curls, her mischievous eyes glinting.

Hanna raised an eyebrow. "You don't seem surprised."

Bee placed the book carefully on her lap. She *was* surprised, but only because this meant her no-horror-in-the-house mom was okay with her getting a signed copy from *the Betsy Chillers author*.

Bee grinned. "You used to live here, didn't you? You didn't just move here, you moved back."

Hanna's eyes grew round from surprise, but she recovered quickly. "That's right. I never thought I'd come back, you know. . . . But time heals all wounds."

Bee smiled. "I think your stories are amazing. *All* of them." She paused, hoping Hanna might say something about meeting a certain girl across the lake.

"Have you ever written a ghost story before?" Bee asked before she could back down.

Hanna readjusted the dried rose tucked behind her ear. "I guess I could never quite decide if ghosts were the bad guys or not. After all, most ghosts linger around because a tiny part of us wants them to, because we still need them. Sometimes ghosts are more like feelings haunting us for reasons we don't understand yet."

Bee pursed her lips, thinking of Alina, who was so much more than a dangerous girl haunting an abandoned lot.

Still, there was no sign that Hanna remembered what had happened, and Bee was about to thank her again for the book and excuse herself, when . . .

"Did you know I wrote my first ever Betsy Chillers adventure here?"

Bee shut her mouth and leaned forward. Hanna's gaze was unfocused, and a single dry petal detached itself from the rose and fluttered onto the table.

"That's right," Hanna continued. "Scribbled down into a diary. But I never got around to finishing it, or even giving it a title. Plus, I'm sure it was horrible." She shook her head and let out a half snort, half laugh. "I hope no one ever reads it."

"Was it about ghosts, then?"

Hanna tilted her head. "Would you call them ghosts? I think for me, it was about something else." She shrugged. "Best friends. Sisters. And magical ginger—"

A holler sounded, followed closely by feet thundering down the dock and a tsunami-level splash, as Mr. Bakshi, Eli, and Lucas cannonballed into the lake to cool off. Bee waited for her cheeks to warm with embarrassment, but instead all she could think of was how fun it would be to join them.

"What am I saying." Hanna chuckled. "I'm rambling on about things that don't make any sense."

Bee tightened her hold on the book, cradling Hanna's gift close to her chest. Hanna didn't remember Alina, but she also hadn't forgotten about her completely, and that was okay. And maybe, just maybe, Bee was going to be okay, too. "Actually, I think it makes perfect sense."

Finally Granny's party was coming to a close, and it was almost as good as going to the Betsy Chillers amusement park. Almost. It was only once all the dishes were emptied and the extra chairs put away that Bee and Lucas had a chance to slip away to the dock.

"So, was the memorial celebration as scary as you thought it would be?" Lucas asked, petting a purring Albus.

Bee reached out to stroke the soft fur, too, wondering whether Lucas had ever planned to tell her that his mom was the author of Betsy Chillers. Actually, it was exactly the kind of thing he would forget to mention.

"It was purrrfect," Bee said.

Lucas let out a snort, which made Bee crack up. It was nice hanging out together, and her chest tightened at the thought of leaving tomorrow.

"You're leaving tomorrow, aren't you," he said, casting his gaze down.

Apparently, she wasn't the only one thinking about goodbyes.

"I guess." Bee walked over to the canoe and tugged it out of the cattails. "But it's not tomorrow yet." She stepped into the canoe with her new book, pulling on her life jacket. "Want to go for a ride?"

The water was like a giant mirror, without a ripple in sight. Bee paddled slowly across the lake, savoring the lowering sun and the last day of her trip. The cicadas sang loudly in the heat and the whistle of flapping ducks overhead forced her to pause and look up. Soon, she'd be back in the city, surrounded by honking cars and beeping pedestrian traffic signals and the rev of city buses streaking by. And also, maybe, there was a small part of her that was stalling. She had struck a deal of sorts with Alina, but would the ghost keep her end of the bargain?

The stink of the marsh rose up as they reached the dead branches of the opposite shoreline, and a series of *plops!* sounded as the painted turtles that had been sunning themselves on the logs dropped back into the water.

"So why exactly are we back here?" Lucas asked, stepping out of the canoe and tying it for Bee. "I mean, we didn't exactly leave on good terms with Alina last night. Will she even show up?"

Bee grimaced as she ducked under the cedars. *You can say that again.* But something told her that Alina wouldn't ignore them.

"She'll show."

The leaves and pine needles rustled over the cobblestones and the yellow stone wall glowed warmly as the sun hit it. A pebble landed on the ground near Bee's feet.

"Bee, Lucas." Alina nodded to them from the top of the wall. The angry lines in her face from yesterday were all but gone. "Albus," she greeted the cat.

Alina hopped to the ground, her feet landing sound-lessly on the pathway. "So, where's the proof?"

Bee cleared her throat, keeping her shoulders back and her chin high. *Nothing to be afraid of anymore.*

"When I first met you, you felt familiar. I knew who you were, even though that wasn't possible." Bee took a deep breath. "Gretta never forgot about you, and Hanna regretted what happened." She pulled the book out and held it in front of her. "In fact, she wrote a whole series about it. You're Betsy Chillers."

Alina frowned, staring at the glossy cover of the girl with long hair and a billowing pirate shirt.

"Betsy Chillers never listens to her parents," Bee continued. "She loves to explore dark and creepy places, gets into all kinds of trouble, and always saves the day. And she has wonderful friends."

A smile flickered on the edge of Alina's lips. She closed her eyes briefly, her dark eyelashes fluttering like moths. "Fine. I promise to never haunt Storm Lake ever again."

Lucas placed his hands on his hips. "How do we know you'll keep your word?"

"The bread crumbs," Bee said, turning to him. "Ghosts can only appear where the bread crumbs are, and your aunt has all of them now." Of course, there was the tiny, itty-bitty detail of the missing diary. . . . She paused, making sure not to break eye contact with Lucas so he understood she was serious. And also to camouflage the last half-truth she ever planned to tell her friend. "So no one else will be haunted ever again."

Lucas scowled. "But *I* still don't trust her. You can't tell me you've completely changed your scary ghost ways."

The dead leaves rustled, and suddenly Alina was next to Lucas. Albus hissed and Bee's breath caught. *Was I wrong to trust her?* But Alina simply brushed a curl from her eyes and lifted a finger to his goggles.

"Hey! What are you—" he started, then stopped, mouth ajar.

Alina stepped back as he peered around, then lifted Albus from his neck. Lucas's face had turned bright red and his lower lip trembled. He then held Albus up, speechless, before bringing the cat's fuzzy nose to his.

"Now you have real ghost specs." Alina sniffed. "You're welcome. See, I *can* change."

Lucas hugged Albus close before letting the cat slink back around his shoulders. Carefully, he removed his goggles. Tears ran down his cheeks. Clearly, the cat's human eyes belonged to someone important, and Bee had a good idea who that person might be.

"Thank you," he said, wiping his eyes.

Alina hesitated, then tilted her head to one side. "Don't mention it." She reached a pale hand out. "Truce."

The cool hand briefly enveloped Bee's, and it felt like dunking her hand in the lake's cold water.

She breathed out a shaky breath as Alina held her gaze. And then Bee and Lucas turned away, and the ghost of Storm Lake watched them solemnly as they got back in the canoe.

Lucas gently petted Albus for as long as it took Bee to paddle them back across the lake. Even though he wiped the tears away, they kept coming.

"What was it like?" Bee asked. "Seeing him again."

Lucas hadn't put the goggles back on yet; they were still pushed up into his hair. "Good." He hiccupped. "Real good. Turns out he's been close this whole time, just in case I needed him."

Bee had always suspected there was something more to Albus, and she was glad her hunch had turned into a happy ending. She recalled the way Albus had led the way through Alina's house and back to Lucas, as though the cat knew exactly what it was doing.

"I would definitely agree with that," Bee said with a small smile.

"Yeah . . ." Lucas turned back to face the front. "Hey, remind me to tell you about my news."

Bee's ears perked up. There was a sudden lightness to his voice, and it felt like the first of many ripples spreading around a skipping stone. "What news?"

"I'll tell you tomorrow."

· 32 ·

Ghost Specs

Bee's parents were fast packers. Years of back-country hikes had chiseled them into machines of efficiency, and their trip to the cottage was no different. By the time Bee stumbled into the kitchen to the aroma of leftover samosa, turned crisp and hot in the toaster oven, the car was fully packed and her dad had tidied up the living room and bathroom.

"Good morning, sunshine." Her mom beamed. "Are you done with that?" she asked, swiping the plate from under Bee's half-eaten samosa so she could finish washing the dishes.

Bee decided to take her samosa outside to the Adirondack chairs, where Granny was quietly sipping her morning tea, floating a few inches from the seat. It was a habit she'd taken up ever since the memorial—floating was a lot easier than walking! The mist was still lifting off the lake, giving it the appearance of some magic brew, and a loon broke the water's surface as it returned from a successful fishing trip.

Granny's large pink sun hat was tilted low over her brow, and it was difficult to tell if she was awake. But Bee knew better by now.

"Good morning, Granny," she said, taking a seat in the deep chair. "How are you feeling?"

Granny tilted her hat up off her face, her white hair peeking out around her temples and her eyes clear. "Bright-eyed and bushy-tailed." She winked as a red squirrel bounded across the lawn and scuttled up the nearest pine tree. "That was some adventure we had the other night, wasn't it? All that running and jumping and fighting off ghosts. We were quite the team!"

Bee took her hand. Granny's skin was no longer dry and frail. Instead, a ghostly strength pulsed there, like when she'd tackled Alina while they were stuck on the merry-go-round.

"We are, aren't we?"

Bee sat there for a bit, watching the lake with one eye and the hummingbirds zipping around the feeders by the wood shelter with the other, until she couldn't procrastinate getting her things together any longer. For some reason, she'd thought Lucas would come by. Didn't he have some important news to tell her?

Bee sighed and brought in Granny's empty cup, stripped her bed, then took her time stuffing her clothes into her backpack. Every few minutes she glanced out the window, until the mist was gone and her mother poked her head through the door. She was wearing her fabulous jungle-print leggings again.

"Are you ready, Binita?" she asked. "We're leaving in five."

Bee looked out the window for the last time. "I'm coming."

A loon's call echoed across the lake and a flash of unruly red hair appeared in her peripheral. *Lucas!* Bee raced out the back door and onto the deck, where he stood waiting by the steps with Albus wrapped around his neck. Bee gasped as she got closer.

"Where are your goggles?" And then she remembered she was a bit cross. "And what took you so long?"

"I know, I know, I'm sorry," he said, dusting crumbs from his cheeks. "But I have a good reason."

"Like what? Snacking on cookies?" Bee huffed.

"About that . . ." Lucas lowered his voice, forcing Bee to lean in closer. "I haven't been snacking, I've been baking." Bee raised an eyebrow. "Auntie Gretta has decided to teach me how to make her special ginger-bread."

Bee's eyes widened, noticing the aroma of ginger and nutmeg coming off his person. "You mean . . ." She nodded toward the lake and the loons that had gathered near the dock. *So that's what they were chatting about so seriously during the party!*

Lucas grinned. "Yup. She's going to teach me everything, so that if there's ever another ghost problem, I'll be able to set things right."

"Wow! That's . . . that's incredible!"

Lucas, an apprentice baker of *magic* gingerbread—it was so incredible that Bee didn't even notice her fleeting twinge of jealousy (who wouldn't want to learn magic?). Before she knew what she was doing, her arms were around him in a big bear hug.

"All that paddling, your arms have gotten so strong, you're squishing me." He laughed, his face turning a deep shade of purple. But Bee knew he was joking because he hugged back.

A cardinal sang in the trees and two kayaks snaked along the perimeter of the lake, passing by the abandoned lot.

"I'm happy for you, really." Bee pulled away as he placed something in her hand.

She frowned, turning over the goggles. "You're giving me the ghost specs?"

Lucas shrugged. "Why not. Thought it would be cool for you. Since I'm learning about gingerbread magic and all, seemed fair. Plus, I don't need them anymore."

Bee nodded, tucking them in her pocket. She knew how much this gift meant to Lucas, and she would never forget it. "Hey, what did *you* see in the cottage that night? What was your biggest fear?"

Lucas passed a hand through his hair, his freckles glowing as his cheeks reddened.

"What?" Bee pressed. "You know my biggest fear now, so it's only fair."

He looked up, meeting her eyes—his were a startling dark green, like a handful of pine needles.

"I don't have many friends," Lucas stuttered. "So I guess what I'm most afraid of is losing y—"

The rude honk of her dad's car rang out, cutting Lucas short.

"I'm sorry, I have to go," Bee said, and before he could see her blushing, she turned and ran up the grassy slope.

Bee grabbed her waiting backpack from the deck steps and flung herself into the car. Granny smiled next to her, surrounded with pillows, the last samosa in hand. The car smelled delicious, partly due to the cooler full of peaches under Bee's feet (Bee had promised to help her mom make more pickle at home, and she was kind of looking forward to it) and the stack of gingerbread cookies on her lap—a parting gift from Gretta.

"Ready?" her mom asked.

"Ready!" Bee said, turning in her seat to take one last look at the lake as the tires began to crunch against the gravel. Then her dad turned left onto the road, and she pulled her phone out and wrote a text.

They wouldn't get reception until they hit the turnoff

toward town, so the message wouldn't be sent until then. But Bee couldn't wait, already imagining Lucas's freckled smile when he opened the text.

You'll never lose me

Content, Bee settled back in her seat as they passed Auntie Gretta's old trailer.

"So, good ol' family time wasn't so bad after all, was it, Bee?" her dad teased.

"You can call me Binita, I don't mind," Bee said, picking the large plastic jewels off her phone until they formed a neat pile on her lap. She opened her window a crack to breathe in as much sweet country air as she possibly could. "And I'll never forget it, that's for sure."

Her mom stretched her hands above her head. "Such a lovely memorial that ended up being. And a lovely week! I absolutely loved it."

"Me too!" Alina said, her shape passing through the car roof and settling between Bee and Granny. She grasped Bee's hand, her dark eyes twinkling. "Thank you for inviting me to your home."

Bee's neck prickled, and she lowered her voice. "As long as you behave. I can just as easily kick you out."

She tapped her waistband, where the final part of their truce remained: the last of the bread crumbs, which Alina had found somehow intact amid the rubble of the abandoned lot—the green diary.

A scowl flickered across Alina's face. "I'll behave! I gave you my word, didn't I? Plus, if you ever want to get rid of me, all you need to do is light a match under that thing and I'll be back at the old house in a flash."

Granny smiled, patting Alina on the shoulder. "Oh, I'm sure we can afford to give *family* a second chance if need be."

Family? Bee rolled her eyes. When she had asked Alina to come live with her, she had meant as a friend. And mostly, she meant it as a way to keep her out of trouble. *Family* was a whole other thing.

Her hands found Lucas's goggles. Maybe it was best this way, though. Alina had never really belonged anywhere, too dangerous and dark and . . . weird. But if weird ever had a home, it was in this family.

It *had* been a good week, and now that it was over, she wished it had been longer. *Who knows. Maybe we'll come back next year.*

"Aren't you going to put those on?" Alina asked, lips curling into a smirk.

Bee sat back in her seat as the car left the crunch of the gravel in favor of asphalt. The last of the pine trees flew by, their shadows flickering across her lap and the otherwise empty back seat.

"Come on." She stuffed the goggles back into her pocket. "You know I don't need them to see ghosts."